SENIOR HEARTS

JOSIE RIVIERA

INTRODUCTION

To keep up on newly released ebooks, paperbacks, Large Print Paperbacks, audiobooks, as well as exclusive sales, sign up for Josie's Newsletter today.

As a thank you, I'll send you a Free PDF ... The Beauty Of ...

Josie's Newsletter

Did you know that according to a Yale University study, people who read books live longer?

5 STAR READER REVIEWS

5 star Reader Reviews:

"Love can occur at any age, even when you think you're too old for " such foolishness ". She was an older elegant widow used to country clubs and European vacations and he was a blue collar truck driver. Can they overcome their differences and self perceptions and biases to find happiness and togetherness?

This is a collection of three such couples all over 50 who carefully navigate a whole new perception of who they are. Josie handles the situations and feelings with tact and grace. As always, clean and wholesome." - **Amazon Reviewer**

"I love this series." - **Amazon Reviewer**

"Love can occur at any age, even when you think you're too old for " such foolishness ". She was an older elegant widow used to country clubs and European vacations and he was a blue collar truck driver. Can they overcome their differences and self perceptions and biases to find happiness and togetherness?

This is a collection of three such couples all over 50 who carefully navigate a whole new perception of who they are. Josie handles the situations and feelings with tact and grace. As always, clean and wholesome." - **Amazon Reviewer**

This set is dedicated to all my wonderful readers who have supported me every inch of the way.

THANK YOU!

DEAR FRIENDS

A heartwarming story is the hallmark of every romance. Savor the magic of seasoned romances with three sweet, clean, and wholesome contemporary stories that celebrate mature couples over 50.

Senior Hearts
3 Books in 1 collection!

Cozy up with your favorite beverage and lose yourself in these fun, joyful romances.

Books included in this collection:

A Chocolate-Box Summer Breeze
Will Emily and Joe find their happily-ever-after in a forgotten summer breeze?

1-800-IRELAND
A strong minded Irishwoman pursuing her dream. A disillusioned businessman ready to retire. Can two deter-

mined people separated by years find true love at the end of a rainbow?

A Chocolate-Box Irish Wedding

A woman who wanted more. A man who wanted her. Can they rediscover their love in the seaside Irish town where it all began?

CONTENTS

A CHOCOLATE-BOX IRISH
WEDDING

PRAISE AND AWARDS

USA TODAY bestselling author

ACKNOWLEDGMENTS

An appreciative thank you to my patient husband, Dave, and our three wonderful children.

ACKNOWLEDGEMENTS

JOSIE RIVIERA

a Chocolate-Box Summer Breeze

CHAPTER 1

*A*t seven o'clock on a Thursday evening, Emily Varon sat alone in a corner booth in Olive's Diner. She swallowed some black coffee, pushed the cup aside and checked her watch.

Joe Vertucci was ten minutes late. Odd, because he was always punctual when he phoned her.

Emily bit her bottom lip, drew back the diner's thick tan-colored curtains, and peered out the window at a sultry California evening. The parking lot was empty except for the few cars that belonged to the customers who were dining inside.

She grabbed her cellphone from her leather handbag and read the last words Joe had texted.

After all these months, I'm looking forward to seeing you in person again, Emily.

Her stomach fluttered as she imagined their reunion. She was looking forward to seeing him too and told him as much. He'd responded with a thumbs-up, which had prompted her to smile. She'd attempted to explain different emojis to him, he didn't always have to use a thumbs-up.

However, he couldn't seem to get the hang of new technology.

Of course, emoji stickers weren't new, and he'd beamed on their video chat when she'd assured that she'd teach him how to use them.

Their only disagreement had taken place when Joe had insisted on paying for their meal. Eventually, she'd conceded and offered to leave the tip.

He'd concluded their conversation with a quip. "That's why I'm crazy about you, Emily. You don't take advantage of me."

Frequently, he'd referred to himself as a blue-color, working-class guy, and she'd heard a trace of disparagement in his voice, as if he was putting himself down. Although people took pride in referring to themselves in that way, she repeatedly wondered if he genuinely believed in himself.

He should. He was a thoughtful, good-natured man.

Again, her gazed flitted to the window. He could have been delayed by rough weather, or unexpected traffic delays. Hazards on the road occurred in seconds, and driver fatigue often caused serious accidents.

Or, perhaps … Joe wasn't interested in her after all.

She rubbed her cheek with the back of her hand, attempting to pry herself free from the anxious speculations. She hadn't dated in years, and her nerves wavered as if she were a schoolgirl.

This isn't a date, she reminded herself, nor a naïve teenage crush.

She opened the menu and scanned the dinner selections. The special featured grilled chicken, and a baked potato, which suited her nicely. However, the diner's delicious coconut cake would surely ruin her diet.

It was her proper upbringing, she supposed, that kept her focused on the latest fashion trends. Often, though, she pondered if there was a reason to watch her weight anymore. The only people she encountered besides the diners were her son and his family, the weekly grocer, her hair stylist, and Sunday morning churchgoers.

A Moonglow Chocolatiers truck pulled into the lot, and Emily's heart leaped. A man with silver-white hair emerged from the driver's side. Several patrons whispered Emily's name, like the murmurings of a breeze rushing through a forest. Somehow, they knew Joe was here to see Emily.

"I haven't seen Joe in a long time." Oliver, the owner of the diner, stepped over to her booth. He held a steaming pot of coffee.

Emily jumped. She was so focused on Joe's arrival that she hadn't realized Oliver had approached.

"You're eating dinner later than usual." Oliver grinned and gestured toward the window. "Are you waiting for Joe?"

"Yes." Hastily, she jammed her cellphone into her purse. "He's overnighting near here for a couple days."

Oliver refilled her cup. "How did you know Joe was in the area?"

"Why are you asking?" She sat straighter and adjusted her flawlessly creased white slacks. Through all her months at the diner, she'd kept her personal life private. "Sometimes, people need to eat dinner with someone else, rather than all alone."

At the swift, questioning look he shot her, she grimaced. Her response had a breathless, edgy quality. "Sorry."

"No worries, Emily, and you're one hundred percent right. I shouldn't pry." Oliver patted her hand. "I can't help being an old-fashioned Cupid, and I detect a romance is brewing."

"Hardly." She dismissed any further inquiries Oliver poised on his lips with a wave. "Joe and I regularly talk on the phone."

"Ever since you met him here in my diner?"

"Yes," she acknowledged. For an instant, she closed her eyes and relived that stormy February night.

After panicking because she'd never been in a situation like that before—stranded in a diner—her nerves had settled, and she'd enjoyed several hours conversing with Joe. The narratives about his over-the-road travels had made her laugh. It felt good to laugh, especially after she had visited with her son the previous weekend. He, his wife, and her grandchild had been cordial, but their life was hectic and Emily had felt useless and in the way.

She knew they loved her, but they didn't need her.

"May I call you?" Joe had politely inquired that evening, after the road had been cleared and the customers could safely leave the diner.

His request had wrung a reluctant chuckle from Emily, but the sight of his incredible smile had done odd quivery things to her pulse.

She'd agreed and wrote her number on a napkin before handing it to him.

Following an exchange of "safe travels", she'd driven back to her large, empty home in town, and hadn't felt quite so lonely.

"I remember you two got along well." Oliver grabbed a cup and paper placemat from an adjacent table and set them across from Emily. "You never mentioned that your relationship with Joe had blossomed. You eat dinner here nightly."

"Your food is delicious."

"Thanks. I might use your testimonial as advertising." He paused. "However, you're not answering."

"Is this a question or a statement?"

"Both, considering I'm an old-fashioned Cupid," he reminded.

"Joe and I are too timeworn for a romantic relationship."

She tasted the coffee, which was always perfect, then dabbed her lips with a napkin. "Even though I gave him my phone number, I didn't expect him to call me."

"Why not? You're an attractive, classy lady."

She shook her head. She wasn't. She'd continually considered herself plump and the opposite of model-thin, but she wasn't about to introduce a lengthy psychological discussion. Plus, she'd been obsessed with tanning salons, believing a tan made her look younger. However, she'd finally recognized that tanning aged her, and had given that up after she'd met Joe.

One didn't need any more wrinkles at her age.

"Thus," Oliver said, "you've been talking to Joe for—"

"Nearly four months. Joe and I believe in phone calls and occasional video chats," she said.

"There's something about hearing a person's voice. It's more personal."

"Yes, definitely. These days, everyone relies on texting." Emily took another sip of coffee. "Young people stare at their cellphones waiting for bubbles to appear when a phone call accomplishes twice as much in half the time. In addition, there's constantly a risk you'll be misunderstood."

In accord, she and Oliver nodded.

"I'm glad he's here now," Oliver said. "Beneath the flannel shirt and jeans façade, Joe is a romantic guy."

Romantic. The idea brought a funny catch to her chest.

Once, romance had made life worth living.

Now?

She lowered her gaze to concentrate on her cup.

She'd lost all sense of romance after Krandall—her tall, striking husband—had unexpectedly died three years earlier. At the image of his well-heeled demeanor, his poise in the board room, his focus and goal-setting ... "I've set my eyes on you, Emily," he'd declared, and the remembrance brought a thickness to her throat. Her moneyed parents had extended not-so-subtle nudges for her to accept his advances so that she could "marry well."

Emily fingered the black-gold and sapphire bracelet, the last piece of jewelry Krandall had bought her before he'd gotten sick.

In fact, he'd purchased many gifts for her, mostly to apologize for his outbursts. He'd been super-critical and continuously chastised her. Sometimes, she believed she was little more than a fixture on his arm that he could show off at high-class fund-raisers.

Glancing up, she realized that Oliver was studying her.

"You're categorizing Joe as a romantic?" she asked him.

"Absolutely. We chatted at length the night he was stranded here, and our conversation was poignant and enlightening."

"Poignant?"

"Guys use fancy words too." He grinned. "From what I gathered, he yearns for a connection with a woman. He was widowed several years ago."

"Companionship … most people are seeking mutual support."

"Joe confided that he longs to feel loved again." Oliver scanned the diner, then set the coffeepot on the table and perched across from her. "Is this a first date? Or a second?"

"Oliver, you're not listening. A widow and widower who are seventy years old don't date."

Although this meeting with Joe was, in every sense of the word, a date. Wasn't it?

No, she repeated to herself.

She fished in her handbag for pink lipstick and a mirrored compact. Ordinarily, she wouldn't fuss as much with her appearance, but the anticipation she'd soon see Joe face to face …

Where is he? the question intruded. It shouldn't take that long to park a truck.

"He's been rummaging for a while." Oliver echoed her thoughts.

Carefully, Emily arranged her silver-blond hair and applied a dab of lipstick. "He keeps track of his hours in a logbook and is doubtlessly making certain the load matches the manifest sheet."

"Manifest sheet?"

"The list of deliveries and shipments." She cast Oliver a sideways smile as he went to the counter to pour two glasses of water.

She'd learned a lot about trucking from her conversations with Joe. What's more, she'd gained an understanding of the man himself. He was frugal, efficient, and fit. He was also sincere, sensible, and because of his job, mechanical.

With an inner sigh, her gaze wandered back to the parking lot.

Tonight was so different compared to the night they'd met. That eventful evening, a severe storm had flattened a tree in front of the diner. Now, four months later, the California rains were nonexistent. Summer bloomed, intense and motionless, the sky a mellow golden hue.

A painter embraced the tints of the sunset, bold tones of orange and crimson. For her, the spectacular evening marked the beginning of another lengthy, desolate season.

Summertime, the potential for light-heartedness and unexpected delight. Days to flaunt straw hats and sundresses, pretty floral blouses, and sandals.

Don't be ridiculous, she scolded herself. The season didn't matter. Not for a grown woman of a particular age.

"What is taking Joe so long?" she blurted, as Oliver returned with two glasses.

"Most likely, he's planning something extraordinary for you."

"From the back of his truck?"

Her thoughts drifted to their conversation the previous evening. As was his custom, he'd phoned at six o'clock, and suggested video-chatting.

"I chuckle whenever I consider Oliver and his diner," Joe had said. "The former owners had named the diner Olive, and Oliver kept the name, declaring it had a nice ring to it."

"Even though we've all told him there's a considerable difference between Olive and Oliver."

Joe laughed. "So let's have dinner together at the diner while I'm in town … the place where it all began."

"Where *what* began?" she'd responded.

"Our … our friendship."

Friendship was a safe word. Although, she'd read in a leading scientific journal that men and women weren't capable of being "just friends" because romance bubbled just around the corner.

Her cellphone buzzed. She pulled the phone from her handbag and checked the screen.

"Who is it?" Oliver stood and plucked up the coffee pot.

Her pulse quickened. "Joe is here. He sent me a thumbs-up."

"I know. We saw him get out of his truck, but now I'm staring at him." Oliver pointed to the doorway as Joe entered. "He looks great. Did he lose weight?"

Indeed he had—twenty pounds and counting. She knew he'd been trying because he'd outlined his nutritious diet, reiterating the calorie and fat content.

And indeed he did. Look great, that is.

Joe's handsome, rugged face was clean-shaven. He adjusted his eyeglasses, then shoved a hand in his jeans, his gaze searching the diner. Searching for *her*, Emily realized with a wide grin.

His manner was comfortable, almost boyish. But it was his genuine, inviting smile, a smile that reached all the way to his blue eyes when he spotted Emily, that encouraged her to grin in return.

She stood, flattened her fine, white linen blouse and hailed him. "His route takes him across the state and back," she informed Oliver.

"Sounds like you're proud of him."

Briefly, she savored the moment as she regarded Joe.

"I am," she said truthfully. "We talk for at least an hour until Jeopardy comes on." Her face sobered. She was showing too much excitement. "Oliver, are you taking note of my social life?"

Oliver chuckled and shook his head. "I can hardly manage my own."

"I imagine that Sally Elliot keeps you on your toes?"

Sally was the woman who owned Bloomingfield Candy Shop. She'd been stranded at the diner that same February night along with Emily, Joe, and several others.

"You're imagining correctly." Oliver wiped a hand on his clean white apron. "I see Sally and her daughter, Clarissa, every weekend. Nevertheless, our busy work schedules produce challenges, because I'm here in Evanville and she's in Bloomingfield."

"Challenges you both are apparently overcoming?" Emily teased.

"For love," Oliver replied, "anything is possible."

CHAPTER 2

*E*mily caught a quick breath as Joe hastened to her table. He carried a package wrapped in blue paper, and she silently groaned, hoping it wasn't another baked good. Thus far, the cupcakes and brownies he'd sent to her had been dry and tasteless.

Joe's bright eyes fixated on her. "My lovely Emily." He laid a hand over his heart, confirming he was as elated about their meeting as she. His voice cracked as he placed the package on the table, then took her hands in his—completely disregarding Oliver except for a brief nod. "Thanks for waiting. I'm sorry I'm late."

"Joe, you're only fifteen minutes late. I'm glad you drive slow and conscientious." She glanced at her watch. Okay, he was twenty minutes late, but that was because he'd spent a few minutes in the back of his truck.

"By the time I finished my deliveries, then sorted the chocolate—"

"Anything on the road can slow your progress," Oliver broke in. "Did you deliver to Bloomingfield?"

"I did, indeed." Joe winked. "Sally said hello. She and her

daughter will see you later this evening when she gets off work. And tomorrow you're both playing hooky in order to take Clarissa to the aquarium at the new mall in Santa Rosa."

"Exactly the plan." A satisfied grin spread across Oliver's features as he wended around the tables, filling cups of coffee for his customers and stopping to chat.

"How are you?" Joe waited for Emily to sit before settling across from her. She appreciated his gentlemanly traits. He was chivalrous in a traditional manner some people labeled as out-of-date.

Emily didn't. Gallant and respectful behaviors never went out of style.

"I'm fine," she replied. "You?"

He beamed, never taking his gaze from hers. "I couldn't be better."

"You're staring at me as though I have food on my chin."

"I was thinking about how gorgeous you are in person. A phone screen doesn't do you justice. And your hair, it's blonder?"

Self-consciously, she touched her hair. Earlier that morning, she'd asked her stylist to color over the platinum silver. After a half hour of consultation and assurances, Emily had decided the two hours in the salon had been worth it.

"What do you think?" she asked. "It's my natural color, minus the years in between."

He chuckled. "I love it."

"I wanted a change."

"It's a marvelous one ... I mean ... I liked your previous hair color too."

"It's not that much different."

He studied her. "No, it's just ... blonder."

Emily tried not to chuckle at how ridiculous their conversation might sound to anyone who happened to listen.

Judging from the patrons eating and conversing, no one had heard them.

Joe nudged the gift toward her. "I brought something for you."

"Chocolates from Sally's shop?" *With any luck*, she thought. Joe was so intent on creating low-fat goodies he'd forgotten that in the end, taste mattered the most.

"Nope," he said. "I baked these German chocolate mini-muffins in my own kitchen."

She kept her grimace at bay. "Are they healthy?"

"Naturally. I substituted unsweetened applesauce for the vegetable oil. The muffins got jostled during the trip, but I re-wrapped them."

Two weeks earlier, he'd mailed her a batch of chocolate chip muffins, followed by brownies. Each time, he used a thin cord of gold ribbon to create a delicate bow. Although stunning to look at, the baked goods inside didn't prove as delicious as the packaging. The last batch had been too sweet, and Emily had tactfully suggested he use real sugar instead of artificial, which frequently left an aftertaste.

He'd agreed, but the following week, his chocolate-coffee muffins had arrived on her doorstep. Those muffins had tasted odd, and she'd (respectfully, of course), urged him to check the expiration dates on the ingredients.

Sure enough, flour had been the culprit.

She glanced up. Expectantly, he watched her as she examined the package.

"Thank you, Joe. You're becoming a baking expert." She smiled.

A little white lie never hurt anyone.

She nudged aside the fake potted lilac plant Oliver always placed on every table, unwrapped the package, and peeped inside. Immediately, she inhaled the aroma of rich, dark chocolate.

"I bought a new bag of flour," Joe said.

She extended a brilliant smile. "Thus you baked two perfect muffins."

Hopefully.

"Maybe not perfect, but I figured that after dinner we'll try them for dessert."

"Joe, you always persevere."

"All I can do is try."

He was sincere and put his whole being into everything. The knowledge caused her to smile. "Oliver's special dessert tonight is coconut cake," she said.

"My muffins have fewer calories than cake." Absently, Joe perused the menu, then grasped her hands. "Is there anything in the world more captivating than you?" he asked softly.

She moved back. "What brought on that compliment?"

"You. Just seeing your lovely face and new hair style."

"New hair *color*," she corrected. "My style is the same." With a laughing sigh, she leaned her head against the green vinyl seat. "There are countless subjects more captivating than me."

"You're not a subject. You're my Emily."

She concentrated on his words. Nonetheless, she drew her hands away and clasped them properly on her lap. They were friends, she repeated to herself, and she wasn't about to get cozy in a public diner. She'd grown accustomed to living life alone, although, through Joe's direct and indirect hints, she intuitively knew he craved more from their relationship.

Joe frowned at her response. There was that directness about him she admired, the way he wore his sentiments on his sleeve. Her late, by-the-book husband had controlled his emotions.

Krandall had been a generous provider, fixating on his net worth and savvy with his fortune, believing the money from his investment business liberated them.

Joe remained silent, evidently waiting for her to say more. When she didn't, he said, "We've established dessert. What is your choice for dinner?"

"I've decided on the grilled chicken special and a bowl of Oliver's homemade vegetable soup."

"Low calorie and hearty, but please choose the most expensive meal on the menu." He held out his palms in a generous gesture. "Remember, dinner is my treat."

"The grilled chicken is the most expensive entrée tonight."

He laughed. "Then I'll have the same, because this is a celebratory evening."

After they'd placed their order with an efficient teenage waitress, Emily leaned in. "Do you eat all your meals in diners, Joe?"

"Usually." Yet again, he grasped her hands. "What about you?"

"I never eat out anywhere but here, and only for dinner. I prepare my other meals at home."

"We should dine together more often. When I'm driving, all I can think about is phoning you from my hotel room. You're the highlight of my hours and I love hearing your voice."

The heartfelt attentiveness in his gaze and the enthusiasm in his tone made Emily feel warm and cherished.

"I feel the same," she said. In fact, his calls had become a lifeline, and she looked forward to telling someone about her day. "Although I wish you'd cut back your working hours—for your sake."

"I can't, Emily. I'm paying off my daughter's college tuition loan because she recently lost her job. As a single mother, Lydia is struggling. She applied at the bank for a debt consolidation and seeks employment every day."

You're struggling financially too, Emily thought, but she didn't share her contemplation with him.

The fact that he was compelled to work an exhausting job in order to pay his daughter's bills brought a sadness, an infuriation, to Emily's chest. By now, Joe should be ready to retire.

Managing his route and the truck's contents while staying on schedule was arduous for a younger man, and ever more so for someone Joe's age. Yet, he managed it all while maintaining a courteous demeanor with his suppliers and customers. Even when describing his workdays he never complained, and she innately knew he wouldn't welcome her observations or sympathy.

Emily blew out a breath. "Your actions are admirable. However, your daughter is a grown woman."

"Wouldn't you do the same for your son? From what you've mentioned, he's doing well financially, but if he wasn't—"

"Naturally," she agreed. "But I wish you would relax more."

"Relaxing isn't a word in my vocabulary." Joe downed his water, then fidgeted. "So Emily, where do we go from here?"

"We? Why? Where are we going?"

For the first time, she questioned if there was another purpose for their arranged meeting that Joe was easing into. Since this was a special and upbeat reunion, she followed his lead. Perhaps she'd shift their discussion to small talk, rather than student loans and debts. At cocktail parties in the past, she'd been a pro at engaging people in light conversations.

"It's a figure of speech." Joe cleared his throat and scratched his chin. "I have the next few days off."

"Good. You deserve it."

"How about you?"

"I don't work."

He scanned her face. "I mean, what do you have planned for the weekend?"

"Nothing."

Oliver wandered to the juke-box, and the jingle of coins dropping in the slot followed as he selected a song, throwing a grin at Emily over his shoulder.

Several seconds later, Frank Sinatra's voice crooned the first few measures of "You Make Me Feel So Young," an upbeat romantic ballade.

She grinned at Oliver and awarded a wave. There was something about being in a familiar place—with an attractive man who was obviously interested in her sitting across the table—that brought an excitement she hadn't envisioned. Add the music, and the night was magical.

"Are you a Frank Sinatra enthusiast?" Joe inquired.

"I love his music, particularly 'Come Fly With Me.'"

"I'm a Beatles fan."

"Rock?" She scoffed. "All the music sounds the same —rebellious."

"Not the Beatles. Their music is fresh and innovative. How about country songs?"

"No, but I adore musicals," Emily replied. "Especially *Cats*, by Andrew Lloyd Webber."

"I've never seen a live musical, nor listened to any."

"You've never visited New York city, or strolled on Broadway?"

"Nope." He sat on the edge of his seat. "What's the musical about? A cat?"

"Several cats, and my favorite song is 'Memory'." With a soft murmur, she called up the lyrics ... "being alone in the moonlight with remembrances of the past."

"Is there a storyline?"

"Of course. The old cat, Grizabella, is mourning her

youth." Emily tipped her head to the side. "Sometimes the older you get, the more it seems like you've disappeared."

Sometimes, oftentimes, she'd felt that way with her son and his family.

"What's your favorite song?" she asked. "Besides anything by The Beatles."

"Give me any tunes by Journey."

"You're going on a journey?"

"Journey is the band's name, Emily."

She offered an abashed smile. "I'm joking."

"I know." He shifted but didn't grin. "Are you spending the Fourth of July with friends?"

She automatically tensed at the question. Any social life since she became a widow was nonexistent. Her core of socialite friends had avoided calling, and Emily learned that several wives considered her a threat because she was single.

To keep active, she'd tried a sip and paint class before concluding she wasn't good at sipping wine or painting. Hence, she'd given up on a night life, or a day life, or any social life, for that matter.

"No plans," she replied.

Joe kept his features reserved, although the affection in his deep-blue eyes betrayed him. "Will you see your son?"

"He and his wife and my grandson are taking a hiking trip to the mountains."

"They didn't invite you?"

"Not in so many words, but I suppose the invitation was there." She kept her voice a monotone. "I'll call him. That is, if he has cell phone service where they are camping. Oftentimes he doesn't pick up. However, I always leave a message."

Joe extended a half-smile. "I do the same."

"Our adult children and their families lead hectic lives."

"Yes."

Emily focused on the ceiling. "Anyway, I've never slept in

a tent before and informed my son that I'm certainly not starting at my age."

"So you prefer creature comforts?"

"Totally. You?"

"Delicious food, a pleasant home, and a delightful woman by my side is my vision of paradise," Joe said. "I could probably climb into a sleeping bag ... however, climbing out is a different matter entirely."

"Because of the zipper?"

"Because I'm seventy." He smirked. "It's not easy for me to get up."

His upbeat banter was so infectious that she grabbed his hand before she could stop herself. "Not exactly a simple task for me, either."

"Unless we're both planning to become Olympic athletes in our seventies, sleeping in bags on the ground probably isn't a satisfactory plan. You're physically fit, though, Emily. I presume you work out."

There was no mistaking the admiration on his features.

Her face flushed. The two-mile walk on the treadmill every morning was tiring, but obviously worth it.

She drew back but didn't release her gaze.

"My daughter and her little girl won't be around either." Joe picked up his coffee cup and smiled at her over the rim. "What I'm trying to ask is ... are you interested in riding to Cambria with me? I'm scheduled to pick up another chocolate delivery near there, but not until Monday. Therefore, my days in between are clear, plus I'm paid for the vacation."

"And you choose to spend those days with me?"

"Absolutely."

"You mean ... ride with you to Cambria ... in your delivery truck?"

"Sure, and we can enjoy the long weekend together. Cambria is a little seaside town. I've visited a number of times because there's a major chocolate distribution center close by. Tourist attractions in Cambria include a castle and a boardwalk, and we can watch the sunsets on Moonstone Beach."

Emily attempted to tamp down her excitement, although her senses reeled. "Where is Cambria?" she hedged.

"About five hours away."

"I'm not sure—"

"No pressure." Joe set down his cup and grasped her hands again. "No expectations. Just two friends taking pleasure in one another's company."

She eyed the Moonglow Chocolatiers truck in the parking lot. "Is there enough room for me?"

"I'm driving a box truck, Emily. There's plenty of space."

"I'm not accustomed to packing lightly."

"Bring whatever is best for a beach trip, especially if it fits into a duffel bag."

She frowned. She couldn't recall if she even owned a duffel bag, but she owned a set of white designer suitcases.

"Fair warning," Joe said. "If I keep any clothes and items in the back, they tend to smell like chocolate."

"Tend?"

"They do. They will."

With a quiet giggle, she assured, "Chocolate is my favorite."

"Me too, or I wouldn't have lasted two decades transporting it across the state."

She pressed her lips together, still debating. "Is there a downside of riding in a truck?"

"Well, dust always lands in the passenger seat."

"Can anything go wrong on the road?"

"Plenty." He caressed her fingers with his thumb. "A punctured tire, a cracked windshield—"

Halfheartedly, she stifled a grin. "Joe, are you trying to talk me into going? If so, you're hardly succeeding."

"Because I saved the best for last." He sat straighter. "My truck has something no other can boast. Besides having you along for the ride, of course."

"Which is?"

"A year ago, I installed an eight-track cassette tape player in the dashboard."

"The proprietor agreed?"

"I leased the truck for five years, and now I own it."

"I commend your entrepreneurial spirit, but where did you find cassettes?"

"Several big-box stores, vintage record shops, and online. It's a niche industry, but many people prefer tapes."

"Therefore, there is no CD player in your truck?"

He quirked a white eyebrow. "What are those?"

"CD's are—" She caught his smirk and joined in. "At any rate, eight-track cassettes are antiques. Like us."

"We're not antiques, Emily. We have an exciting life ahead of us and an entire world to experience."

She shrugged. "Maybe." She wondered exactly where that world was located … sometimes. At other times, she was content in her quiet, daily routine.

Wasn't she?

Of course.

Moreover, repetition was excellent for aiding memory, and her routine was invariably the same. She drove the short distance to the diner for dinner, conversed with the other customers and Oliver, and returned to her comfortable brick house in the center of the small adjacent city.

Rinse and repeat, her conscience chided, noting that her days had become repetitive and dreary. Was Joe's invitation an opportunity for adventure?

"What are the accommodations in Cambria?" she asked. "Are there hotels?"

"There are numerous motels and hotels and quaint bed-and-breakfast spots. At last count, Cambria's population was around six thousand."

"You described a seaside town." Emily envisioned starfish, tumbling waves, and a smart pier harboring million-dollar yachts.

"Cambria is near the Pacific Ocean," Joe continued. "The community boasts an abundance of sea life, including otters and seals. We can book a boat excursion if you'd like. I did once when I was there … by myself." He paused. "We can swim, although parts of the coast are rocky."

Emily's head came up at the swimming reference. "Decades ago, I was a member of my college's swim team."

"What was your best stroke?"

"The backstroke." She met his gaze. "Were you on the swim team in college?"

"I didn't attend college, but I know how to swim. To support my family, I took the first job offered as soon as I graduated from high school. My father had died when I was young, and my mother cleaned houses for a living. We constantly struggled to make ends meet."

When she didn't respond, Joe granted a broad, disarming grin. "May I confess something?"

"Why not?"

"I rented a tiny, quaint cottage by the sea. It's not as fancy as the deluxe resorts where you vacationed when Krandall was alive." He hesitated. "I know you summered in Europe and wintered in the Bahamas."

She shook her head. "Contrary to what you might presume about me—"

"You prefer the finer things in life."

"Admittedly, but Cambria sounds enchanting."

Joe blinked. His eyes rounded. "My tiny cottage will suffice?"

"Nicely." She bit back a smile at his enthusiastic tone. "However, if you've already rented the cottage, then you assumed I'd agree to your invitation?"

"I wasn't certain." He squeezed her hands. "Nonetheless, I was hopeful."

She turned to the window. Night had descended, the golden colors of afternoon had dimmed to twilight, then blackness.

And there was one more subject to resolve.

"Joe, without sounding prudish …" She subjected him to a delicate raise of her eyebrows. "We both were married, but my mother instilled Victorian values in me that I still ascribe to."

"Excellent." He grinned. "Your mother must have known my mother."

When he continued to grin, Emily reiterated with utmost honesty. "Consequently, I won't share a bedroom with you."

"I respect you too much to ask otherwise. The cottage I rented has two bedrooms, and I'll sleep in the smaller of the two."

CHAPTER 3

*W*as this beach trip a wise idea?

The following morning, Emily pondered the question while she finished packing. She'd selected casual, comfortable clothes. After all, it was a spur-of-the-moment invitation. For the drive, she opted for a black and white jersey knit sundress, black leather sandals, a thin silver bracelet, and a cardigan sweater to drape over her shoulders.

When had she last gone on a vacation, or anywhere at all since Krandall had died, except to visit her son and his family?

Pausing to rest on the tufted sofa in her cozy sitting room, Emily set the duffel bag on a table and drew a knitted blanket over her lap. Because of the air conditioning, she was often cold.

She leaned her head back. Too excited to sleep the previous evening, she'd risen when stars still flickered in the sky. She hardly ever slept well anymore, waking frequently.

After their dinner at the diner, Joe had phoned when she'd returned to her house, describing in enthusiastic detail the places in Cambria she might be interested in—the charming boutiques lining the boardwalk and an artifacts gallery displaying art painted by local California artists. She envisioned a Nantucket-style cottage, a coastal retreat with lattice greenery growing over the roof. A sunny, gleaming oasis decorated with cane chairs and needlepoint pillows.

A thumbs-up text from Joe brought her to her feet. She stifled the kick in her pulse as his truck rounded the street corner.

A minute later, she was partway across the living room when the doorbell rang. Although she was overjoyed to see him, she was determined to stay poised and attempted to tamp down her enthusiasm as she opened the door.

He stood on her front steps with his hands dug in the pockets of his khaki shorts, wearing a smile that revealed white teeth. His strong pride showed in his rough-hewn features, and the firm mouth that had tenderly kissed her goodnight.

He wore sunglasses, quickly pointing out they were prescription when she complimented him on his appearance.

He held her hands in his, then slanted his head. "How much stuff are you bringing?"

"Stuff?

"Clothes ... stuff."

"This and that. Somehow, I managed to fit most of my toiletries into a duffel bag."

"Somehow? Almost?" He peered around. "I don't see a duffel bag, but I do see two large white suitcases."

"My duffel bag is in the sitting room."

"Sitting room?" He shoved up his glasses. "What's that?"

"A place where you ... sit. I needed something slightly bigger and couldn't fit all my clothes into one little bag."

"A duffel bag expands."

"Not enough," she countered. Because she'd added another one-piece swimsuit, a cover-up, two more sundresses, nightclothes, a bold pearl necklace, white cotton slacks, and a couple flowery-print blouses. In addition, her makeup and night clothes took up more space than she'd anticipated, which had necessitated the second suitcase.

Joe rubbed his temples. "I'll store your suitcases in the back. Be ready to smell like chocolate when you open them in the morning."

"You warned me already, and I'm prepared." She hung her hands on her hips, opting for a more logical approach. "What woman can fit all her weekend outfits into a duffel bag, anyway?"

"Certainly not anyone as fashionable as you." He placed his arm lightly on her shoulders. "I phoned my daughter. Did you speak with your son?"

"He seemed pleased I had plans for the holiday." *Immensely, overly pleased.*

With a twinge of heartache, Emily had detected her son's relief. Definitely, she was joyful because he had a devoted wife and an adorable son, but oftentimes she felt abandoned.

"Excellent." Joe brought a hand to his forehead and peered toward the hallway. "Are you ready?"

"Whenever you are." She retrieved her duffel bag, secured the windows and snatched her purse, and house keys.

Joe lifted her suitcases and feigned an amplified groan. "Imagine if we traveled for a week. What would you pack then?"

"Enough for at least four suitcases." At his incredulous stare, she quickly inserted, "Just kidding."

As they walked to his truck, he paused to regard her. "I still can't believe I persuaded a fine, wonderful woman like you to come along with me."

"It was the eight-track cassette player," she reminded with a laugh.

He opened the passenger door, then waited as she

climbed in and buckled her seat belt. "Thank you for agreeing to ride with me, Emily. This trip means more than you can imagine."

"Me too," she said quietly.

He was a thoughtful man with a tender heart, and she hardly was able to contain her happiness that she'd met him.

He started the ignition and eased onto the street, then the interstate, while Emily fiddled with the radio stations. When the disc jockey's voice introduced the next song as country/western, a man in an SUV pulled up next to them at the stoplight. His SUV blasted the same station.

"My cassettes are in the glove compartment." Joe had evidently noticed Emily's pained expression as Willie Nelson blared from their twin speakers. A woman, apparently, was always on Willie Nelson's mind.

Emily sifted through the row of cassettes—ranging from The Eagles to an assortment of Beatles collections—and her hand stilled. "Frank Sinatra's Greatest Hits? The soundtrack from *My Fair Lady*?"

"I couldn't find the musical you mentioned … the one about dogs."

"Cats," she corrected. "And I thought you didn't care for—"

"This morning, I patronized an oldies store in town."

"You were searching for music for me?"

"Only for you," he said affectionately.

She was special to him, and the knowledge filled her with delight.

The miles passed rapidly, and Joe remarked on the numerous tourist attractions. Traffic moved at a crawl when they hit construction sites, and he braked slowly and gently. Whenever they picked up speed, acceleration was seldom quick.

"We're in Bloomingfield," Joe announced when they drove

along the main street of a charming town. He angled his steering wheel toward the curb. "This is where Sally Elliot owns her candy shop."

"Don't stop," Emily said. "Sally isn't working today because she and Oliver and her daughter are visiting an aquarium."

"Oh, right." Joe stared out the front window and carefully merged into traffic. "Her sister, Julie, owns The Pasta Junction, a fine Italian restaurant here in town, and she makes her own pasta. Her eatery doesn't open until dinnertime, though. Have you frequented either place?"

"I don't travel much farther than the diner," Emily answered with a broken laugh. She shook off her defeatism and said graciously, "But Oliver's food is tasty."

"His meals are the best in the state," Joe agreed. "We'll stop in Bloomingfield some other time, alright?"

"Alright."

He glanced at her. "Is that a promise?"

"Indeed." Emily nodded and stretched out her legs. Her limbs felt weightless, and her expectations were positive.

Some other time. A promise of a next time.

"I've never ridden in a truck before," she confessed. "I'm up so high."

"There's a first for everything, and the view is better."

"Is driving difficult? The ride is a bit rough, and I noticed you swing wide on your turns."

"Yep, and I take ramps and curves unhurriedly."

For the next half hour, they covered an expansive stretch of highway while serenaded by Frank Sinatra's soothing voice singing, "That's Life." Up ahead, a billboard advertised a fast-food restaurant at an upcoming exit.

"Are we stopping for lunch?" Emily asked. "I'm content eating at a drive-through."

"I packed sandwiches," Joe replied. "Or rather, the deli prepared them. There are several roadside picnic areas."

"I haven't picnicked since ... forever."

"The spot where I'm headed is on a riverfront."

"Krandall preferred to dine at the country club," Emily mused.

"Nothing against a country club, although I've never even entered one. I prefer to eat outdoors. Food tastes better, particularly a classic turkey sub with roasted red peppers, which I requested especially for you."

She clutched her fingers together. "How did you know some of my favorite foods?"

"Easy." He chuckled at her reaction. "I phoned Oliver. I ordered the same sub for myself, except I requested mine garnished with green peppers instead of red."

When they broke for lunch, she heartily agreed that food tasted better alfresco, further declaring she was becoming a nature lover. To her surprised pleasure, she wasn't immune to the ambiance of an unassuming meal and devoured an amazingly marvelous lunch. As she reached for a cold bottle of water from the sack of drinks and sandwiches, she marveled at the backdrop of their location—the grove of redwood trees, the rushing river, and the scenic, towering mountains.

They disputed whether green or red peppers were tastier, and she did fun things—simple things—such as sitting by the river and skipping rocks.

"Find the smoothest, flattest rock," Joe instructed, demonstrating that a simple flick of the wrist produced the best bounce. "Also, face the water."

"Where else would I face?" She laughed out loud, relishing the friendly competition as she thrust rapidly and the rock flew airborne.

"Next time, I'll teach you how to spin rocks," he said. "You're certainly a pro."

"My newfound skill," she jested, "is skipping rocks."

"You beat me on every throw."

She shoved the hair off her forehead, her lips twitching with laughter as she embraced the finest, most relaxing day she'd ever experienced.

But of course she was with Joe, and as she'd previously determined during their numerous conversations, he had the ability to change ordinary events in life into memorable ones. No fancy meals for him. Just plain old-fashioned fun that didn't rely on a high-priced atmosphere or over-the-top chef creations.

Afterwards, Emily lounged against the truck while Joe filled the tank with gas. She relished the soothing breeze against her face and the brilliant glow of the afternoon sun, grateful for the straw hat she'd worn to protect her complexion.

In a few short hours, they exited the highway. The day had flown by, and soon they arrived at the cottage. Emily rushed across the stone walkway, taking in the appeal of the classic Cape Cod style—the weathered cedar shingles and white wooden shutters.

And then she stopped.

The cottage looked neglected, as if it hadn't been updated in decades.

"The website stated that the cottage had a run of owners, but the reviews were pretty good," Joe said. "Plus, the rental rate was reasonable."

Pretty good. Reasonable. Emily made a quiet groan in her throat. Half of the dilapidated wrap-around deck faced the shimmering Pacific ocean, and two rusty pink bicycles sat propped against an abandoned rose trellis.

"I haven't ridden a bike since I was a teenager," she

murmured, sidestepping the fact that the bicycles screamed for a major repair, as did the rest of the property.

"Neither have I." Joe gestured to a younger woman who stood on the sandy beach and stared at them. With his arm draped around Emily, he steered her toward the doorway and tipped her chin up. "I bet our neighbor thinks I should kiss you before we enter our weekend escape."

Emily tucked her hands at her sides. "I bet she's not thinking any such thing. She doesn't even know us."

He lowered his head. "Let's show her what two happy people look like ... two people on top of the world."

Emily bit back a helpless smile as their lips touched. "Make it quick," she murmured.

"I can't kiss you quick when you're laughing."

"I'm laughing because you are."

As their breaths merged, he extended a friendly wave to their neighbor.

THE MUSTY, dry odor of the cottage's interior hit Emily first.

"This place was advertised as sparkling clean and boasting divine beds," Joe muttered.

"Nothing that an airing can't solve," Emily chirped. "We'll open the doors and windows."

They stepped on creaky, white-washed wooden floors and came upon the larger of the two bedrooms. A red and white buffalo checked quilt covered the single bed. An ancient air-conditioning unit blocked most of the cracked window, and slivers of light shone through. Outside, rolling sand dunes, and tall grass swayed in a wind gust.

"If I owned a cottage in a splendid location like this," Emily said, "I would remodel the bedroom, install central air-conditioning, and let the sunlight in. The view of the ocean is spectacular." She ran her fingers over the dusty oak veneer chest and studied a watercolor depicting a fisher-man's boat set against a backdrop of jagged cliffs. Embla-zoned in blue letters on the boat's stern was *Summer Breeze.*

"Sometimes, owners name their boat after a pleasant memory," Joe remarked.

"Summer Breeze brings to mind hope and joy. It's easy to forget any concerns with the promise of summer to cheer you." Emily balanced on her toes to examine the initials etched in the right-hand corner. "K. S. Who do you suppose that is?"

"There was a Keaton Smith art gallery in town a few months ago when I was here," Joe replied. "Let's include the gallery on our itinerary."

"I like itineraries." Emily offered a smile, then reluctantly returned her attention to the bedroom, particularly the cobwebs. Her smile faded as she pondered how long it had been since the walls had absorbed a fresh coat of paint, or the four rooms had been filled with the aroma of a Sunday pot roast.

"When you stare at the floor," Joe said, "you make me think the cottage is inadequate."

Quickly, she shook her head. "No, no, not at all. It's lovely …really. Only, I'd anticipated something more modern." Belatedly registering his wounded expression, she focused on a point over his shoulder, regretful for allowing her expectations to prompt her to blurt her reservations aloud.

Several seconds of unpromising silence followed.

She stiffened, expecting a verbal set-down. When Joe didn't respond, she encouraged, "Please talk to me. I'm sorry."

"What would you like me to say?"

"To begin with, you can chastise me about my comment."

"I'd never chastise you."

"Okay, but you can tell me that I was rude and ungracious."

"I won't do that, either." He sighed. "This is a cottage built in the 1920s, Emily. You can't expect modern. I told you it was quaint."

"I realize you tried to find the best place on a budget." She drew a long breath. "Are you upset by my remark?"

"I'm not sure."

"I don't understand."

"When it comes to you, my thoughts haven't been clear since we met. In addition, my insecurity grows heavier every second we're together." He kept his stare downcast, which prompted Emily to smile.

She rattled him because he was attracted to her.

"I'm thrilled to hear that," she declared.

Joe didn't appear nearly as thrilled. He rubbed the back of his neck, sat on the edge of the bed, and invited her to sit beside him. "We should come to a clearer understanding of what is happening between us, and, more importantly, how we should continue."

"Joe, we just arrived. This conversation is too serious."

He steepled his hands. "Shall I speak first, or you?"

She flinched. He'd ignored her statement.

"Go ahead," she relented.

"Fifty percent of the time I shake myself, a reminder that I'm really here with you and this isn't all a dream," he said. "You're too attractive and elegant to devote your days to a guy like me."

"Don't put yourself down. I respect you a great deal."

"We're not having this conversation because I'm fishing for compliments, Emily."

She fingered the silver bracelet on her wrist. "And the other fifty percent?" she prodded.

"Despite how well you may perceive me and my lifestyle,

I'm a galaxy away from being inexperienced. The perfectionism I strove for in my youth, the same perfectionism I believe you still want, disappeared for me many years ago. We're both seventy and should acknowledge our differences. I'm the opposite of a wealthy millionaire. I earn an hourly wage and will never receive a six-figure, end-of-year bonus." The grin had long since vanished from his features. "This isn't a senior prom, and I'm not speculating about whether I'll kiss you, because I already have, and—with your permission—will do so again."

Her cheeks heated. He was frank about expressing his feelings. She liked that.

Politely, she folded her hands. "Are you finished?"

"Should I be?"

"Can't you understand that I'm proud of you and what you've accomplished?"

"I own a delivery truck, Emily, and my house is a quarter of the size of yours."

Their earlier excitement was rapidly disintegrating, and an imperceptible strain slowly descended on the tiny bedroom.

"Those things aren't important to me," she replied.

He tapped his fingers on his knee and didn't look convinced.

She inhaled and smiled. "Well then, everything is settled."

"What's settled?"

"You have my permission."

"For what?"

She peered at the doorway. "It's been nearly a half hour since you kissed me and …"

Realization dawned on his face.

Smiling, he cupped her chin and silenced her next words with his lips. As further proof she was sincere, she flung her arms around his neck and returned his kiss.

Several minutes later, they walked hand in hand through the narrow hallway to inspect the galley kitchen, which was painted a dark cobalt blue and boasted glass cupboard doors.

She scanned the chipped Formica countertop. "Where's the coffee machine and pods?"

"There is a coffee pot on the stove." He indicated a stainless steel percolator, then stepped to the white refrigerator and peeked inside. "I also arranged a grocery delivery for necessities."

Sure enough, a quart of milk, a dozen eggs, a loaf of bread, butter, bottled water, and ground coffee perched on the top two shelves.

"You planned everything." She darted a glance at the shabby surroundings, forcibly reminding herself that this was a beach cottage, not a five-star resort. "Where is the bathroom?"

"It must be through here." As he freed a jammed door, his voice went quiet. Water leaked from the sink's faucet, and the mirror reflected tarnish. Although only one person at a time could fit in the cramped space, the tiles gleamed and fresh white towels hung on the towel bars.

She peered inside. "There's no shower stall."

Joe strode to the living room and grabbed a brochure off the coffee table. "I read about an outdoor shower, but I assumed it was to rinse off the sand after a day at the beach." He swung wide a saloon-style door in the kitchen which led outside.

"Hmm."

"Hmm?" she asked.

"I guess the shower is truly outdoors." He hesitated before facing her. "I assume that's okay … because … because you're a nature-lover, right?"

CHAPTER 4

*N*ature, Emily soon realized the following morning when she stepped into the outdoor shower, presented a challenge. And clearly she wasn't a nature-lover after all.

Spiders and creepy-crawlies naturally gravitated to a damp area. In addition to the leaves and sand piled in the corner, clouds rolled in while she was soaking wet and the wind picked up, leaving her shivering and taking the fastest shower of her life.

And then there was the bigger problem.

In addition to the compactness of the space, she was *exposed.*

Not to mention that she had to hang her rosy-red sundress and clean undergarments on the door and hoped they didn't fall into the dirt while she quickly scrubbed herself. Thankfully, the warm water, plus the fragrant euca-lyptus spearmint soap she'd brought from home lifted her spirits.

She didn't bother with make-up except for a pastel pink lipstick, foundation, and mascara. She had secured her neatly coiffed hair with a shower cap beforehand so it didn't get wet, and later swept back the ends with a thin, glossy-red headband.

Despite the obstacles, she was determined to impress Joe.

Why did she care about impressing him? she challenged herself. They were two friends sharing a weekend. Romance wasn't part of the equation. Furthermore, there was no attraction between them.

Hah, her conscience chided, and she thrust it aside. Oftentimes, her conscience was an annoyance.

A half hour later, fully dressed and made-up, she slipped on easy, closed-toe shoes and entered the kitchen.

The front door and windows were wide open, and the weather promised a silvery-blue sky and comfortable temperatures. Emily caught a whiff of a salty sea breeze and the echoes of percussive waves hitting rhythmically against the shore.

Joe stood near the stove, brewing coffee and popping bread into the toaster, and his efficient movements made her smile. The attractiveness of his robust physique, his purple polo shirt tucked into navy shorts, hastened her breathing. Feeling suddenly shy, she shoved her hands into her pockets and wished him a cheerful good morning.

"Good morning, beautiful." He met her smile, and her heartbeat doubled at the affection in his gaze. "Red becomes you."

She braced her fingers on the counter and took a slow breath. *Friends, friends, friends*, she reminded herself.

"How was your shower?" he asked.

"Quite an adventure." *Talk about an understatement.* "A stunning sanctuary isn't the first description that comes to mind."

"The second?"

"Um, no. Perhaps airy?"

"Therefore, the experience was ..."

"Harrowing. And my clothes smell like a chocolate factory."

"I warned you." He grinned. "I encountered a large spider."

"That's all?" She laughed, then feigned disappointment. "You were lucky."

"Why? What did you see?"

"The better question is ... what *didn't* I see?"

He barked with laughter. "I rose before dawn and showered early."

"I didn't hear you."

"You were fast asleep. Did you rest well?"

"Surprisingly, yes. I opened my window and the sound of the ocean waves lulled me to sleep. Usually it takes me a long time to fall asleep."

"Me too, but not last night. It must be those divine beds." She giggled her assent as he reached into the cupboard for mugs and poured two cups of coffee. She inhaled the deep, rich aroma.

"You take your coffee black, right?" he inquired.

She nodded and relished the first sip. Of course he'd remembered her preference.

Standing, she spread butter on their toast, and they worked companionably, bantering while they set their dishes in the sink after a light breakfast.

"No dishwasher," he murmured. "Sorry."

"I can certainly wash and dry a few dishes. There's nothing to apologize for." She glanced his way and her pulse quickened. Her feelings for him multiplied the more hours they spent together.

"Let's venture into town and stock up on more food supplies," Joe suggested. "I want to try a new recipe while we're here."

"Another brownie that promotes weight loss?" Emily teased.

He draped a dishcloth over his shoulder and perched his hip at the edge of the table. "Lydia emailed me a recipe for peanut butter bars. She insists they're delicious." He pulled out his cellphone and scrolled.

Emily eyed the tiny stove, and oven, then peeked over his shoulder. "All my favorite ingredients. Butter, peanut butter, and chocolate."

He frowned. "Hardly low-calorie."

"Excellent news." Emily placed the last of the clean plates in the cupboard. "A modest amount of fat isn't necessarily bad, as long as you balance the foods with a nourishing meal plan."

He didn't appear convinced but tucked his cellphone into his pocket. "This afternoon we can visit William Randolph Hearst's castle. I reserved two tickets for a tour of the grand rooms."

CHAPTER 5

A few hours later, as the tour guide detailed the history of the magnificent Hearst Castle, Joe scanned the gardens, then concentrated on Emily. With her hair pulled back by a red headband and a hint of pink lipstick on her full lips, she presented a stunning vision. Her complexion was clear, and her heavenly blue eyes were framed by black lashes and elegant eyebrows.

"Can you believe the castle took all those years to finish?" Her demeanor was upbeat, and her gaze shone with excitement as she pointed out the architecture surrounding the opulent pool.

Joe nodded. "Right."

"From 1919 to 1947! And building on the mountaintop in order to capture the breathtaking views was brilliant. I am in awe of Mr. Hearst's vision."

Again, Joe nodded.

She squinted and slipped on her sunglasses. "Hence, you agree?"

"Yep."

"Uh, huh. Did you hear what I said?"

"Of course."

She hung her hands on her hips. "Tell me, then, word for word."

"You began with … we're on a mountaintop." He continually lost his train of thought as he gazed at the curves of her figure, her stunning smile, and the sun shining on her face.

"Therefore, you weren't listening. First, I remarked on the views because they are awe-inspiring." She drew in a breath. "I wonder what the rooms that were not included on our tour look like."

"You do?"

"Yes." She paused, and he sensed an uncertainty in her voice. With any luck, she was exploring a dignified way to suggest another road trip with him.

"You'd like to see more of the castle?" he encouraged. "With me?"

"Am I that transparent?" Studiously, she observed the rose bushes and avoided his gaze. "You must realize you're the ideal—"

"Companion?" He drew her nearer and chuckled, the scent of her spearmint fragrance uplifting. Steadying himself, he pondered why she had such an insane effect on him. "You're my ideal companion too."

She hesitated and pulled at the neckline of her dress. "Joe?"

Whenever she uttered his name, her delicate, pure voice had a dreamlike quality that stirred his senses.

"Hmm?"

"I'm glad we met."

"Me too." He held her close. "I believe fate has a hand in these things—how people meet, when they meet. Sometimes events take place that are beyond our control."

Slightly, her lips parted. "Fate is from the Latin word, fatum, which means 'that which has been spoken.'"

"Did you study Latin in college?"

She rested her head on his shoulder and grinned. "I read a lot, but I learned that from Webster's Dictionary."

THE REMAINDER of the day was a blur of shared hugs and a peaceful walk on the beach. Later, a stroll through town revealed that the Keaton Smith Art Gallery had shuttered a few months earlier. However, they appreciated the sense of originality in the flourishing community that especially beckoned to Emily. She stopped often and browsed—particularly at the stalls where local jewelers created white polished necklaces, rings, and matching bracelets, and crafters wove bright-colored quilts.

She purchased a nautical souvenir for her son's home, plus a bag of caramels for her grandchild, and Joe did the same.

When an antique dealer invited them inside his shop, Emily murmured that his pieces seemed ideally suited to the cottage's ambiance.

"You mean because they're old?" Joe jested.

"Nothing can be as old as that cottage," she solemnly returned.

Simultaneously, they both laughed.

He hugged her then, right in the middle of the shop. He couldn't get enough of her, which was a unique experience for him. Since his wife had died a decade before, he'd found little claim in socializing because no woman appealed to him. Sure, his friends arranged double-dates, but Joe had made up his mind. He wasn't interested in anyone or anything except his daughter, his grandchild, and his work. Any dreams before his beloved wife's death had been lost.

That is until now.

Emily fit effortlessly in the curve of his arm. She was

appealing, curious, and captivated him with stories about her experiences traveling around the world—Europe and Asia and Africa—places he'd never envisioned outside of magazines and television. In her enthusiastic style she'd encouraged him to imagine new possibilities again.

He'd also been impressed by her understanding of technology when she'd adeptly showed him where to find the emojis on his phone. That had resulted in a half hour of experimentation as he'd texted her pink hearts, red hearts, dazzling hearts, and an array of golden stars that had prompted her to giggle until tears streamed down her cheeks.

Sometimes she was stubborn, other times she charmed him with her smile. She was refined and elegant, never showy, topped with so much love bottled up that she mesmerized him.

"All my life I've lived for my son," she said.

"Live for yourself, not others," Joe replied. "Although it's entirely understandable when it comes to our children. They are an important part of who we are."

Emily's eyes had glistened with tears. "There are instances when my son is too preoccupied to spend time with me and I miss the noise and clatter of a crowded household. I remember when I believed the outside world was fraught with peril, and my mission was to protect him."

"You describe memories I also hold close to my heart," Joe admitted. "I miss those years too."

He was living proof of that emptiness. It was the main reason why he preferred to be on the road—to avoid going home to a desolate, lonely house.

Although he and Emily were the same age, he was a million times more world-weary, because he had grown up in a poor neighborhood, whereas her life had been one of affluence. Nonetheless, something about her relaxed him, and that was novel.

However, she avoided any discussions about their future, explaining she didn't wish to ruin their hours together with talks about anything other than the present. Besides, they were too old for any of "that foolishness."

The foolishness of love?

Or was she ashamed of him, his modest background and line of work, and too considerate to vocalize her feelings? He was suitable for a fun, light-hearted weekend, but beyond that … nothing.

He'd always been a plain, unassuming guy, accustomed to simplicity. At eighteen, he had taken the first job that had come along and was grateful. He'd noticed Emily's barely disguised disapproval when he'd mentioned assisting his daughter financially and couldn't understand why it seemed to upset her. At his stage, he was pleased to help his family while they were down on their luck. In addition, he'd managed to tuck away a fair amount of savings.

ON SUNDAY, Joe spent the afternoon assembling ingredients for the recipe his daughter had sent. Emily came and stood beside him in the kitchen and assisted. As a team, they creamed butter, spooned in the peanut butter, and measured the oatmeal.

After the peanut butter bars finished baking, they assembled a tray and two mugs of herbal green tea and headed into the living room. The only TV displayed a makeshift antenna, and they caught tidbits of black and white Andy Griffith Show reruns, which suited them nicely. The everyday activity of passing time—relaxing and watching TV with a special woman—was something he hadn't enjoyed in years.

As Emily placed the half-eaten tray of cookies on the

coffee table, he spoke with a grin. "I decided I prefer regular butter over the low-fat stuff."

"Hurray and don't forget extra chocolate." She stood to brew more tea. As he observed her walking gracefully to the kitchen, he admired her effortless, natural style and the understated sophistication in which she carried herself.

At his insistence, she'd dressed up for their Sunday together. She'd strung a large pearl necklace around her elegant throat, and her deep-blue sundress matched the color of her vivid eyes. With her shiny hair pushed back, her face radiated a sun-kissed glow. After getting ready, they'd found a white-steepled church in town and attended services.

After the service, he'd caressed her cheek and kissed her.

"Tomorrow is our last day," she said, and he detected the conclusiveness in her tone. Or perhaps he imagined it.

"Unfortunately, yes," he replied, his voice shaky. "But we have several hours together while we pick up the delivery, and the ride back home."

He envisioned her attending various social functions when she was married to Krandall—charity balls and Broadway musicals in New York City, and couldn't imagine how he'd forgotten that he'd never be a part of those scenes. He wouldn't escort her to extravagant events because he couldn't afford them. Furthermore, his awkwardness would embarrass her.

In that instant, he understood that not having her in his life was going to be hard, but there was no other choice. Emily deserved better than anything he could offer.

Vacantly, he focused on the paneled wall in the living room as a hollowness filled his chest.

"What are you thinking?" she asked, returning with two steaming mugs.

"Nothing." He shifted. *Nothing he would share with her.*

He offered his best imitation of a smile. "Shall I bake the

next cookie batch using spray butter and artificial sugar?" He suspected that she didn't care for his low-calorie baked goods. She'd never told him, not in so many words, but oftentimes a person conveyed more by what they didn't say, rather than by what they did say.

"No! Please!" Emily sputtered, almost dropping the mugs before setting them on the table.

"I can save several hundred calories—"

"At the expense of taste."

"I've lost weight since I lowered my calorie intake," he loftily responded. "However, this is our vacation, so I'll just sit on the couch and eat more cookies." He gave her a sidelong smirk, snatched a cookie from the tray, and took a bite. "Although the middle is undercooked."

Emily nestled closer, and he shared his cookie with her. "Blame it on the tiniest oven in the universe, not your daughter's recipe."

"Are you saying … never blame the cook?"

She laughed and lifted her lips to his. She tasted of chocolate and sweetness and all that he'd missed for so many years. "Never, ever blame the cook."

"Emily, you're the best thing that has happened to me in a long time," he whispered. "Always remember that."

If she wondered why he'd uttered that last part, she gave no indication. Instead, the bonus for his admission was a dainty brush of her fingers against his chin, and a kiss that stole his breath away.

SEVERAL HOURS LATER, they rode in his truck to Moonglow beach and strolled the planked wooden walkway of the boardwalk. Along the way, they searched for moonstones. Yes, there were really moonstones, he assured Emily, and many people made jewelry with them—such as the necklaces and rings and bracelets they'd admired in town. As they found shiny black pebbles and polished sea glass, they often rested on the benches lining the pathway. Joggers ran past, riders on bicycles flew by at a brisk clip, and a couple stopped to converse—describing the playful seals they'd spotted earlier in the day.

As Joe and Emily continued, an easy summer breeze ruffled Emily's hair, and the tang of the ocean filled his nostrils. Fingers entwined, they admired the rock-strewn cliffs and jaw-dropping coastline.

"We didn't have time to take the boat excursion," he said. "Or to swim."

"Maybe next time."

He turned to gaze at the ocean, his heart heavy, knowing there would be no next time.

One last night together.

He wanted all that they were sharing—tomorrow, the day after that, and the day after that. He longed to paint the town red… would she know that old expression? He suspected she would.

He yearned to embrace life and celebrate every hour with her, because time went by too quickly.

She snuggled against him and he squeezed his eyes shut for a moment. Nearby, people threw red, white, and blue confetti in the air, waved American flags, and cheered.

He soaked in the ambiance of the enchanting pint-size community, its gentler pace, and the way the sun scattered bits of golden sequins on the Pacific Ocean. Fireworks marked the July Fourth celebration, and patriotic music blasted from a loudspeaker in the distance.

A flood of affection, of contentment, radiated through him.

He loved their little cottage. Unquestionably it showed

maturity, but the weather-beaten shingles proved it had lived successfully through another season, despite its age.

Much like him. Much like Emily.

He loved this ageless place that hinted at a kinder lifestyle from a date long forgotten.

And then he realized what he'd known in his heart all along.

He was in love with Emily Varon.

CHAPTER 6

*S*unrise came quicker than expected, and Emily snuggled under the buffalo-checked red and white quilt longer than she'd planned. A sea wind whistled through the cracks of the window as she reluctantly opened her eyes.

They were leaving.

Quickly she showered and then packed, appreciative of the coffee and toast Joe had placed on the oak chest in her bedroom. When she tried to swallow, the coffee tasted bitter in her constricted throat, and the toast was dry and flavorless. A disturbing awareness hit her, setting in motion sadness and confusion. She didn't want to return to her private and solitary existence.

Making a concerted effort to maintain her composure, she pondered why this trip with Joe had come to mean so much.

However, she couldn't let him know, choosing not to appear needy. Especially when she suspected that her son and his family considered her clingy and desperate.

She finished arranging the last of her toiletries in the duffel bag and stepped to the doorway. The Moonglow

Chocolatiers truck idled, exhaust coiling densely from the tailpipe into the sultry morning air.

"Good morning, lovely." Joe adjusted the emerald-green silk scarf she'd tied carelessly around her throat. "Are you ready? I brewed an extra thermos of coffee for the ride, and I included leftover peanut butter bars to nibble on before we stop for lunch."

Emily bobbed her head, but her legs refused to move.

"There's rain in the forecast. I'll need to drive slower and keep my lights on." He peered at the gray clouds on the horizon, then hoisted her suitcases.

"Okay. I'm in no hurry." Emily went into the kitchen and slowly picked up the coffee pot, disposing of the coffee grounds and washing the mugs and plates they had used. She held Joe's mug against her heart, tracing the rim with her finger before she placed it back in the cupboard.

With a muffled sigh, she glanced around. Much as the cottage was in disrepair, she would truly miss the place.

After they collected the cases of chocolate at the delivery center outside of town, the rains started. Joe kept the radio volume low and made no mention of playing any cassette tapes. He increased his following distance and checked the truck at a deliberate, safe speed.

After an hour, he pulled into a rest area, and Emily grabbed the thermos and poured them coffee. They stood under a tree, and a car sped past, splashing water against the truck.

Hazardous weather. Rain. Construction. Joe was under a considerable amount of strain, regularly driving under challenging conditions, and this had been his occupation for countless years.

They stopped several more times for gas and food, and the mood remained solemn.

They made it through Bloomingfield an hour later than it

had taken to cover the same distance in sunny weather. Soon, they would be back in her hometown.

As they covered the last stretch, Emily sat straighter and gathered her courage. She'd never declared her feelings openly, certainly not to a man she'd known for mere months.

Nonetheless, the time had come.

She couldn't envision a life without Joe, couldn't accept the agonizing awareness of resorting to repeated phone and Skype calls with him again.

Despite her jittery stomach, she dismissed her reservations and single-mindedly focused on one objective. She didn't care anymore about sounding needy. In truth, she *was* needy when it came to continuing their relationship. And she would tell him, employing her 'small talk' finesse.

"Joe?" she began.

"Hmm?" He kept his gaze forward, the wipers beating a recurring back-and-forth flap against the windshield.

"I'd like a more permanent courtship."

So much for finesse.

He blinked. For a split-second, he took his gaze off the road and regarded her.

"How? I constantly work, Emily."

"Perhaps you can drive less." She took a quick breath. "Or, preferably, not at all."

"I need to continue working, Emily."

She pushed on, crossing and uncrossing her legs. "Move to my town, so we can be together more often."

"You're talking marriage?"

"Well—"

"In summary, I'd have no income and would rely on your money to support me?"

"I didn't say that."

"I noticed you didn't ask to move in with me. I assume you're ashamed of my house, although you've never seen it."

His shoulders curved forward as he concentrated on the road. "Let's face it, Emily, you're ashamed of *me* because I'm a common truck driver."

"You're misconstruing all my words."

"Am I? What would my daughter reckon, and my fellow drivers, if they learned I was with you? They'd suspect I was after your wealth."

"You assume this is about money, and you're worried about your self-esteem?" Letting out a shocked gasp, Emily sat back. "It's about a full-time relationship rather than a part-time one. I deserve better than that."

"You deserve better than *me*," Joe countered. "Someone who fits into your world."

She flinched, and her stomach hardened. As they passed Olive's Diner, she stayed silent. When they arrived at her house, Joe parked the truck and came around to open the door for her.

"Thanks for coming with me," he said briefly, and leaned forward.

In case he wanted to kiss her, she held up her palm to ward him off.

He grimaced, grabbed her suitcases and duffel bag, and carried them into the living room.

"Thanks, Joe. Goodbye. Safe travels." Her chest hitched. She couldn't say more.

His grimace remained. "Goodbye, Emily." He stumbled back a few steps, then spun. Without another word, he got into his truck and drove away.

CHAPTER 7

*S*even days went by. Then fourteen.

Despite her efforts to occupy herself, Emily pined for Joe, missing him desperately. He'd sent a brief text saying he was driving to another part of the state and would be gone for a while.

And then, nothing.

Naturally, she was too proud to phone him, and awaited a call that never came. Obsessively, she checked her phone and waited.

The weekend they'd shared had begun like a fairy-tale. Oftentimes, she imagined another scenario, a happier ending. If only their relationship had turned out differently.

Yes, she loved him, and believed he cared for her.

But now it was over.

ON A TYPICAL THURSDAY evening a week later, she sat at a corner booth in Olive's Diner, staring out the front window at the sunset. Fresh pink and tangerine orange colors ignited the sky. The month of July was coming to a close, and the days had been reduced to a smudge of summer. She'd gone into town more often, holding on to the breeze as she chatted with people she passed. It felt wonderful not to disconnect from strangers anymore.

She'd even enrolled in a painting class again, surprising herself when she discovered that she did better when she put forth more effort. Her earlier lack of talent had grown from mental obstacles, and she'd been hesitant to try anything new since Krandall's death for fear of failure.

Failure was a matter of one's experience, she supposed. The fear of risking her heart and subsequently losing it, had almost broken her. That is, until she'd relaxed her tight muscles, taken a fortifying breath, and stepped into the art studio again. Her first attempt had produced a watercolor of a fishing boat, which she'd proudly hung on her sitting room wall. On the stern, she'd penned, 'Summer Breeze' in scripted calligraphy. In addition, she'd filled her home with vases of pink and yellow seaside daisies, a display of cheerfulness she seldom felt.

Oliver stepped to her table, bringing her musings to the present.

"The air-conditioning broke," he said.

"I noticed it's warm in here tonight, but I don't care for air-conditioning, anyway."

"Have you seen Joe lately?"

She swallowed hard. "No." They'd been over this every day since she and Joe had parted.

"Are you ordering tonight's special?" He grabbed a pencil from behind his ear and tugged an order pad from his apron. "I'm serving lasagna."

"Excellent. I expect the pasta is loaded with extra ricotta cheese and heaps of calories."

"Guaranteed." He tapped his pencil on the edge of the table and peered at his watch. "Look, Emily. I wanted to surprise you and probably should have told you earlier, but—"

"Lasagna isn't a surprise, Oliver." She gazed at him with frustration. "You serve lasagna on alternate Thursdays." She glanced out the window and her head jerked back as a familiar Moonglow Chocolatiers truck pulled into the parking lot.

"It's about time," Oliver muttered, perching across from her. "He's running late."

She grabbed Oliver's arm. "It can't be ... Joe is in town?"

"We've had nightly conversations, and I knew he was coming this evening to see you."

Her heartbeat accelerated as a short, handsome man—carrying a package wrapped in blue paper and a thin gold bow—strode into the diner.

His usually neat flannel shirt puckered at the waist, his white hair was disheveled.

"When did you arrange this?" She squinted at him. "How?"

Oliver set the order pad on the table, a doodling of two hearts in the corner. "I'm an old-fashioned Cupid, and recommended he take action."

"Hi, Emily." Joe strode to her booth. Tears were in his eyes as he hesitantly set the box on the table. "I brought you a gift."

She stared up at him. "Joe, if it's brownies ..."

"I think I'm done playing Cupid." Oliver shoved to his feet and moved to the counter. "Shall I prepare two servings of lasagna?"

Emily regarded Joe.

"Absolutely," he agreed.

Still reeling, she said stiffly, "You could have mailed the package, Joe."

"I'm not here to deliver brownies." He settled across from her, gazing at her with boyish eagerness. "I'm here to offer you what's in this box."

"Did you bake another low-calorie recipe?"

He shook his head. "Not low calorie. No calorie."

"What?" She couldn't help herself. She was staring at him.

"Please open it."

She did, and then she gasped. A polished moonstone ring, exquisite in its simple luminous beauty, was set in a magnificent gold setting.

"I wasn't sure of your ring size. However, the jewelry maker in Cambria assured me that the size can be altered."

"You bought this in Cambria?"

"I ordered it ahead, left my house before dawn and picked it up this morning. The way we parted ... it's not over. *We're* not over. I traveled halfway across the state to be with you."

"Five hours each way. That's a long drive."

"Not for the woman I love."

He loved her and was uttering the words out loud. The knowledge made her breath catch.

His voice was deep and gripping. She'd longed to hear from him, to see him.

"All this effort ... for me." She fixed her hand on top of his. He was warm, animated, dynamic.

"Our life together," he said. "There's a wonderful, exciting world waiting for us to explore."

She opened her mouth, and then closed it, celebrating the upcoming years in her mind.

He pressed his fingers to her lips. "I want to marry you, Emily, and I won't take no for an answer."

"You said you didn't want to be with me. You were

concerned about what your daughter and co-workers might assume."

"I'm ashamed of myself, because it was my own self-esteem and fears that caused the problem. I couldn't allow people to speculate that I was with you for your money. I would never use you."

"Joe, I don't care about other people's opinions."

"But I do, and I will protect you from any disparaging remarks because I love you, Emily."

"And I love you."

"Good. Good." He beamed. "I've spent many hours pondering our situation, and I figured out a workable solution."

She nodded, waiting for him to continue.

"I'll drive part time, and when I go on a trip, you'll come with me."

"But, Joe, where will we live?"

"Anywhere." He paused, then grinned. "I have nowhere to go, though, because I sold my house. However, I managed to purchase a quaint cottage in Cambria with part of my savings. It boasts an outdoor shower and is situated near the sea."

She pressed her fingers to her throat. "You bought our cottage?"

"Yep. It needs a painting, though."

"I can paint."

The infectious grin that had filled her days in Cambria settled on his features, along with a charismatic trace of conscience. "I approached the owner who was more than willing to sell for a fair price. He even threw in the two bicycles at no extra charge."

"Generous." She shared his grin at that. "What about my house?"

"Keep it, sell it. We can discuss the logistics later."

"After living there for thirty years, I'll sell." She gazed up at him with a helpless smile. "I expected to never see you again."

"Yet, here I am." He pushed up his glasses. "Will you marry me, Emily Varon?"

"Yes. Yes. Yes." For the first time, she noticed the stubble of his white beard, the strokes of weariness at the corners of his bright-blue eyes.

He secured the ring on her left hand finger, then leaned over and kissed her, gently and lovingly and expressively. She curved her hand around his nape, and he buried his kisses in her hair. From the corner of her eye, she spotted Oliver placing a cassette tape player on the counter.

"Now?" he asked Joe when they pulled back from their kiss.

Joe turned to Oliver. "Perfect."

The poignant music from Andrew Lloyd Webber's musical, *Cats,* floated through the diner. The handful of patrons looked up from their meals and smiled. Apparently, the entire diner was in on her surprise.

Emily's heart tightened. "That's my favorite song. 'Memory'."

"I found the cassette online, and I've listened to the music ever since."

"You discovered musicals," she said.

"Especially the lyrics to this song. You're not alone, Emily. Not in the moonlight, not in the daylight. We're here, together, living for today and tomorrow. We'll create our own memories."

She glimpsed Oliver opening several windows to let in a flurry of air, and then her gaze settled on Joe.

The man she loved. Their journey in unison.

"We'll create our own life events," Joe was saying.

And the beckoning of a summer breeze, lighting the landscape of their lives.

The End

A NOTE FROM JOSIE

Thank you for reading *A Chocolate-Box Summer Breeze.*

I wanted to write another story centering around the characters in the "Chocolate-Box" series, and chose an older couple—Emily and Joe—to share a summer romance with you.

If you loved this sweet romance as much as I loved writing it, please help other people find *A Chocolate-Box Summer Breeze* by posting your review.

A Chocolate-Box Summer Breeze is available in ebook, Paperback, Large Print Paperback, Hardcover, and Audiobook.

I'd love to meet you in person someday, but in the meantime, all I can offer is a sincere and grateful thank you. Without your support, my books would not be possible.

As I write my next sweet or inspirational romance, remember this: Have you ever tried something you were afraid to try because it mattered so much to you? I did, when I started writing. Take the chance, and just do something you love.

My Spotify Play List for A Chocolate-Box Summer Breeze is here.

With sincere appreciation,

Josie Riviera

Love the "Chocolate Box" sweet romances?

Be sure to check out the other books:

Click here.

RECIPE FOR LYDIA'S PEANUT BUTTER BARS

#1 CRUST:
    1 cup margarine
    1 cup brown sugar
    ½ cup white sugar
    4 cups oatmeal
    Mix together, PRESS in an 12 x 18 ungreased pan.
    Bake 375 degrees for 12 minutes. COOL.

#2 Spread over crust.
    1 cup creamy Peanut Butter
    (Place in the garage or outside to harden.)

#3

12 – 18 ounces of chocolate chips

1 ½ - 2 Tablespoon butter

Melt together. Dot evenly over peanut butter and spread out.

#4

COOL. Cut into squares. **Place into a cookie tin or a plastic container.**

Refrigerate. Keeps well for up to a month.

Enjoy!

USA TODAY BESTSELLING AUTHOR

JOSIE RIVIERA

1·800 IRELAND

A SWEET CONTEMPORARY NOVELLA

CHAPTER 1

*W*hy did I decide to do this? I must've been madder than a box of frogs.

Kathleen Kelly nodded politely while listening to Candee, her Realtor, although she scarcely paid attention. While she tried to come up with an animated reply, her mind spun. She hoped she hadn't made the biggest mistake of her life.

I'm in America. I've done it.

Meanwhile, Candee gushed on and on about Roses, their picture-perfect North Carolina town. Voted one of the best places to live by a national magazine, Roses frequently persuaded travelers passing through to sell their homes and relocate there.

Kathleen grinned, because she was one of those travelers. However, she hadn't passed through Roses. Her Dublin hometown was 3600 miles away.

The internet was a marvelous thing, connecting people from all around the world. Finally, after months of preparation, her dream of owning a business had become a reality.

Cause for celebration?

In truth, she'd been full of starry-eyed dreams and didn't

know what to expect—this being America with its laid-back style. However, she'd found that professionalism and punctuality were respected here, judging by how efficiently Candee had handled the real estate closing.

She eyed the run-down exterior, the broken-down wooden front door that looked like it had once been painted turquoise. Moss flourished beneath the eaves, and numerous shingles were missing. The brick façade was crumbling in several places.

This wasn't Betty's Diner anymore. From here on in, this was her place: Kathleen's Teahouse.

Critically, she assessed her reflection in the smudged plate-glass front window. She'd swept her red-gold hair up at the crown, and pinned the overly long ends back from her face. Tired lines etched the corners of her dark eyes, and the blush of color she'd applied along her cheekbones had disappeared, leaving her complexion pale. Her lips, which she'd always deemed too full, looked a tad solemn.

Despite the sunny day, she'd dressed in a suede skirt, thick black tights and ankle boots.

Budding leaves on the tulip magnolia trees whispered of spring, and buttery-yellow daffodils had begun to open. So different from Ireland, where hawthorn hedges wouldn't bloom until May.

"So, what do you think of your new business on Pine Cone Lane?" Candee asked.

"Everything is brilliant, absolutely brilliant," Kathleen lied effectively. Sometimes white lies were best to hide her reservations because the place wasn't nearly as brilliant as all that.

In its heyday, the former greasy-spoon diner had served countless meals, the floors and countertops spic and span. However, it had been boarded up in recent months, which was why she'd snagged the place at a steal before the building went into foreclosure.

With a silent groan, she estimated the number of weeks it would take to sand and repaint, outfit the kitchen and hire staff, and the numerous unexpected details that would surface.

She came up with months, not weeks, although she reassured herself there was no point in olagonin'—whining and complaining—because it only made things more difficult.

However, since she'd arrived in America, being anxious had become her forte.

The long weeks of anticipation and tension had taken their toll and kept her awake at night, and she could think of nothing she'd like better than a tub soak with the lavender soap she'd brought from Ireland. Followed by a lengthy, leisurely nap.

Resignedly, she knew a nap would be out of the question for a long time.

Perhaps forever.

She paused to stand back, surveying the building. If she thought objectively rather than with her emotions, she understood that she wouldn't be able to accomplish everything by herself, especially within a five-week timeline.

She'd scheduled her grand opening on St. Patrick's Day, deeming the date fitting and appropriate.

She envisioned painting the shingles a serene shade of soft-green, overstated by a burgundy-striped canvas awning, much like the awning gracing The Ground Café, her former employer's coffee shop in Dublin. And she wanted outdoor seating on the patio, allowing customers to dine at wrought iron tables beneath vintage-style Edison light bulbs.

Curb appeal. That's what the place needed.

She focused on which project she would dive into first—the interior or the exterior.

She was weighing the pros and cons when Candee asked,

69

"You're not having second thoughts about moving to America, are you? I realize it's a huge undertaking."

"Of course not," Kathleen said. "Ireland was getting a little too small for me."

At thirty-five years old, her mantra had become *pursue my dreams or bust*. Besides, it was too late to check out, things being what they were. Her former coworkers knew she was embarking on a refreshingly different chapter in her life, and it would be disheartening to admit defeat.

Kathleen fidgeted with the gold watch on her wrist, a going-away gift from her employer, Danny Brady.

"Also," she continued, "baking and the restaurant trade are second nature to me. I've spent half my life managing a coffee shop."

Candee covered Kathleen's hand. "Sometimes a fresh start is as simple as buying a dilapidated building and getting on an airplane."

"Did I say that?"

"Oh, and much more, because you not only said it, you did it," Candee said. "You've created your dream life."

Kathleen shook her head. "I used to be smart and sensible."

"In the present circumstances, you're even smarter," Candee said. "And you're strong and beautiful. The first time we Skyped, I couldn't get over how put together you were. You'd already composed a business plan."

Kathleen offered a brittle smile. "Don't believe everything on your computer screen."

"Positive thinking, plus action, leads to accomplishment. You're a doer."

"Despite what my so-called friends advised," Kathleen replied.

"Weren't they supportive?"

"Aye, in a polite sort of way. They gave me rock-hard,

unsolicited advice." For some reason, her thoughts kept darting back to Ireland, and a sense of isolation rolled through her. "They wanted to protect me from making a mistake."

She longed to tell someone about the successful closing of her new property, the deep-blue sky gracing the warm Carolina days, the way the sweetgum tree branches swayed in the pleasant morning breezes.

But there was no one to tell. Danny and his wife, Clara, were busy with their own lives, with a wee one on the way.

"You'll love Roses, and I predict your teahouse will become a tea emporium," Candee said.

"What in the world is that?"

"An emporium is a retail store selling a variety of goods."

"I plan to serve food—Irish tea and scones, sandwiches and cakes. I'm not a chain of fancy shops."

"Well, you should be. Also sell tea and teapots, because you and Roses are poised for success. I can feel it."

Kathleen smiled. Aye, Roses was enchanting. The once sleepy town was thriving, and the lush green grass packed neatly between the brick sidewalks reminded her a wee bit of Ireland.

Except that it wasn't …

Remembrances of lyrical brogues brought a poignant yearning to Kathleen's chest that stopped her cold. She hadn't realized she'd be so homesick. With her accent, she'd already found that oftentimes her words got misheard and misunderstood, and she'd had a hard time communicating even though everyone spoke the same language—English.

"This area will get a lot of foot traffic, especially on warm spring and summer evenings," Candee said. "Here in the Carolinas we enjoy a temperate climate, so don't rule out winter or fall, either."

"Unlike Ireland." Kathleen chuckled.

"Does it truly rain buckets?"

"Our term is bucketing down," Kathleen said, repeating the standard Irish joke. "Although the rain is at least warm in the summer."

Candee laughed. "Is it windy?"

"Not much." Kathleen lifted her shoulders in a teasing shrug. "Except small children and pets are sometimes blown clear away to England."

"Believe me, you'll enjoy the weather here," Candee concluded with a laugh. Gently, she urged Kathleen to the diner's doorway.

Kathleen blinked at the dazzling noon sunlight and realized her stomach was growling. She hadn't eaten anything except a slice of her homemade Irish brown bread when she'd woken at six a.m.

"What do you think of your upstairs apartment?" Candee asked. "Internet photos don't do a place justice, but housing above your teahouse is a money saver. You won't have to pay rent nor commute."

"Aye. Although truth be told, it's all in a little worse shape than I expected."

"Manageable, though, I trust?" Candee's puzzled frown swung from the door to Kathleen. "I realize it needs curtains."

"It lacks a lot more than updated curtains," Kathleen said with a laugh. "And it will take an army of crewmen to get everything in working order by St. Patrick's Day."

"My husband, Teddy, is a contractor. He'll get the place turned around for you in no time." Candee shook back a strand of red hair that had come loose from her braid, exposing a pair of gold cross earrings, the only jewelry she wore except for her wedding rings. Even without an ounce of makeup, the woman was stunning, her green eyes gleaming whenever she discussed her husband and their adopted son, Joseph.

In addition to being a Realtor, Candee had opened an afterschool daycare facility in her home for disadvantaged children in the community. On several occasions, Kathleen wondered how Candee was able to do it all. She'd been inspired to match her stamina and ambition.

"As long as there's running water, a kitchen and a bathroom in my apartment," Kathleen said, "my needs are met."

"Good. Your reference from Danny Brady was excellent, by the way."

"I never missed a day of work."

"And he said your brown bread flew off the shelves whenever it was featured."

"He granted me the option to take my recipe to America, and I ran with it."

"Free and clear?"

"Danny understood I was drained. After countless years as his head assistant, I wanted a change." Kathleen wished the warmth burning her cheeks didn't give her away. Why couldn't she compartmentalize her second thoughts like she did everything else in her life?

Because she was excited.

And mildly terrified.

"I expect he and his wife will come to America and visit me someday," she finished.

Candee studied her. "So, at present, you're alone."

"Aye." Kathleen considered saying more, to explain she always felt lonely despite her attempts to build relationships.

She kept her lips sealed. Some words were better left unsaid.

In a little over two years, she'd been duped by a man not once, but twice. First, by a moneyed Italian she'd met on the internet who had turned out to be, surprise, surprise, a young boy. And then, Alexander, an American businessman, had played her for a muppet—a fool.

Danny Brady and his bodyguard, Ian, had said Alexander was too talkative. Talkative? Hah! What an understatement! Charmer was more like it, and Alexander was so smooth-talking he could sell ya an eye out of your own head. He'd had her believing he was genuinely interested in her. When she'd fallen for him, his charisma had changed to controlling. He'd quickly become domineering and expected her to be subservient.

As Candee continued to study her, Kathleen offered, "The man I believed I loved was actually two different men. He was fine as long as things went his way and I was passive." She shrugged and tried to act unconcerned. "Although being submissive isn't in my nature. As I advanced in my career, our relationship quickly fell apart."

"You said you wanted a fresh start, and you've created it. Here's to new men and extraordinary opportunities." Candee gestured to the doorway.

"I'll take the opportunities minus the men," Kathleen said. Truly, she was done with con men, eejits—idiots—who expected women to take a back seat to them and their opinions. Men who exuded personality while keeping a close watch on their own agendas. Men who fired off derisive comments for no other reason than to feel superior.

She was a woman who had helped Danny Brady's Ground Café achieve fame. Here and now, with determination and hard work, she'd make her teahouse a noteworthy addition to this quaint little town.

"During our Skype sessions, I mentioned that your teahouse will offset Keiran O'Malley's Irish pub nicely." Candee pointed to a side street. "His building isn't far from here."

"Keiran's cousin, William, first spoke of Roses and recommended you as a Realtor, which is why I messaged you," Kathleen said. "Fortunately, I zoomed in on this town fairly quickly."

"William lives in Dublin, right?"

"He also knows Sean, my coworker from The Ground Café. Both men wanted to date me, and I turned Sean down flat."

"And William?"

"He frequented the café a couple times a week. We dated for a short while after my breakup with Alexander until I realized I wasn't ready for a romantic involvement." Kathleen swallowed, giving herself a breather before continuing. "Sean still texts me now and then. He wishes to come to America to help me with my new business."

"Is that a good thing or a bad thing?"

"I'm not certain. Sean is competent, but I can't imagine he'd actually fancy working for me. He and I were on the same level as managers." She exhaled. "At any rate, William had told me that Keiran loves it in Roses."

"He's married to my sister, Desiree. They are extremely happy."

"I've heard."

Happy. Such an elusive term.

"Keiran said that life called him back to Roses. Maybe the town called you here too."

Kathleen reflected on Candee's words. She'd read about life's calling in self-help books and tuned in to endless podcasts on the subject. Sometimes, it seemed like she'd waited her entire life for a voice to explain which bend in the road led to happiness.

Nevertheless, if one's calling was a voice whispering in her ear, she hadn't heard a sound. Perhaps a calling was the Lord tapping her on the shoulder. Either way, she'd known in her gut that Roses was the ideal spot, and everything had clicked into place.

"In any case, here I am," she replied.

Candee opened her arms, firmly clasping them around Kathleen. "And this is the dawn of the grandest adventure of your life."

Tears welled in Kathleen's eyes—a mix of joy, fear, and reservations. She'd chosen her destiny, following in the footprints of the Irish immigrant.

Don't be an eejit, her inner voice chided. *You're launching a teahouse, not fleeing from a potato famine.*

"And I can't wait to introduce you to everyone," Candee said. "Desiree and Keiran, my husband Teddy, and our son, Joseph—"

"Aye. When the time comes." Now she was sounding standoffish.

She drew a see-through container from her leather shoulder bag. "Before I forget, I baked a loaf of my brown bread for you this morning."

Candee stepped back. "You haven't been here two days and you're already baking bread in your apartment?"

"I ran the oven before I even unpacked." She handed the container to Candee. "This is a thank-you gift for taking care of the million incidentals that came with an international real-estate transaction. And, for fixing up my apartment before I arrived."

"My pleasure. Decorating is my thing, and you advised me on your likes and dislikes. In fact, you were quite decisive."

"I don't have much of a knack for it."

"Oh, but you do."

Kathleen envisioned the packing boxes strewn throughout her flat's hallway, the luggage and clothes piled by her bed. She should have put away her belongings a while ago. Instead, she'd drawn on a ruffled apron, let a batch of dough rise, and baked.

"Take a bite," she urged.

Candee obliged, closing her eyes as she nibbled. "This bread is one of the best baked goods I've ever tasted. And that's saying a lot, because my friend in Miami owns ..."

"I plan to sell Irish brown bread every day," Kathleen said, grinning broadly at the compliment. "Although I'll need to sell more than bread."

"What about pizza?" Candee asked.

"I'll leave pizza to the pizzeria in town. Presently, I'll turn my energy into outfitting the bakery with delicious Irish desserts and an array of tea selections. In Ireland, people aren't in such a hurry. We savor every moment, and I intend to create the same experience in my teahouse."

"Unlike America," Candee said.

"Comfy couches and free Wi-Fi," Kathleen went on. "Brewed tea in a variety of flavors—chamomile, mint, and a host of exotic herbal leaves."

Her ideas overflowed. Were they too ambitious?

"Have you set your hours?" Candee stooped down at the doorway, muttering about the weather stripping not being sufficiently tight to prevent air leaks.

"I'll open at eleven, and close by nine at night."

"You realize you're describing ten-hour work days?"

"Aye." Like a shot, Kathleen's brain worked rapidly. "I'm still on the lookout for locally sourced ingredients so I can serve healthy salads, sandwiches, and wraps. For dinner, stone-baked pita bread topped with goat cheese and caramelized onions will be a nightly special."

Candee linked arms with Kathleen and walked to the side of the building, where rickety exterior stairs led to the second floor. "What you're describing is enough work for twenty people. And that pita bread sounds a lot like pizza."

"It's Irish pizza, so no competition with the local pizzeria." Deciding on her menu options, Kathleen hardly realized Candee had come to a determined stop while saying a man's name twice.

Rob. Rob.

"Who is Rob?" Kathleen asked.

"He's a dear friend and owns a string of popular bakeries." For some reason, Candee's pitch heightened. "His chain is called Rob's Marvelous Muffins and is based in the Miami area where he lives. He's delightful and funny and easy-going—"

"Brilliant, I'm sure." Kathleen went back to the menu choices in her mind. Irish bacon and poached eggs, or a traditional Irish breakfast complete with roasted tomatoes and mushrooms? Perhaps beef burgers and cider glazed salmon for lunch.

No. She reined in her thoughts. This wasn't a full-scale restaurant.

"I'll begin advertising for employees soon and start with a modest staff," she said, "Did I tell you I won't be serving alcohol?"

"Yes, and I applaud your decision."

"Thanks. I've had enough of that in Ireland. People going out on the lash and stumbling home in the wee hours." Kathleen waved a dismissive hand. "I'll leave the drinking to the pubs."

She looked back on the intervention Clara Brady had staged for her alcoholic brother, Seamus. Little good that had done. Once a person was addicted, it was often a long road to wellness.

"What are the requisite number of ovens for a bakery?" Candee asked.

"Certainly a small commercial oven, plus a full-size convection oven is necessary. Also, a deck oven for layer cakes and breads." Kathleen frowned as she considered all the equipment yet to purchase. "Where will I buy a mixer and a—"

"You'll need someone knowledgeable to advise you. Fortunately, Rob has extensive retail bakery experience. He studied at a prestigious culinary school in Florida offering lots of hands-on experience." Candee plucked her cell-phone from her purse. The excitement in her voice matched the glow in her eyes. "He was voted Miami's most successful entrepreneur, and he's just the right person to help you."

Whoever this Rob was, he'd be overwhelmed when he saw what needed to be completed in five weeks.

Unless, of course, he was a miracle worker.

CHAPTER 2

"*R*ob's Marvelous Muffins." Realizing both hands were a sticky mess from rolling out pastry dough, Rob Taylor answered his cell-phone, then balanced the phone against his shoulder. His gaze landed on the commercial mixer on the counter. He switched it on to prepare twenty batches of cupcakes.

Mondays weren't usually hectic, but with Valentine's Day over and the forthcoming St. Patrick's Day holiday, baking green cupcakes galore became the blueprint of the day.

Pushing out a sharp breath, he wiped his hands on the white apron tied around his protruding waist, trying to remember how many cupcakes he'd tasted that morning. One. Well, no, at least two. Okay, three, although the third had lacked his bakery's signature Irish Cream liqueur glaze.

He eyed that same liqueur set near several pounds of unsalted butter by the commercial mixer, ticking off the items on his to-do list. Next, dozens of cupcakes needed frosting.

A diet was in order, but he'd made peace with that long ago. A man owning a half-dozen bakery shops couldn't resist the smell of mouth-watering chocolate, succulent blueberry, or tart lemon muffins. At least, *he* couldn't. And there was nothing to do except, well, keep tasting.

"Rob, are you there? Hi. It's Candee."

He grinned. "How's my favorite daughter-in-law?"

"Umm, are we all of a sudden related?"

"Your husband is like a son to me." Rob silently motioned one of the bakers to shut off the timer going off on a convection oven. "So if Teddy is my son, then you're my daughter-in-law."

"I've always loved your logic, Rob." Candee chuckled. "How's the muffin business?"

"Busy. Can't complain." He muffled the phone as an employee wearing a company hat and sporting nonslip clogs ran past looking for the espresso. The featured cupcake was a combination of flour, sugar, espresso, and that Irish Cream liqueur.

"How is everyone in Roses?" Rob asked. "Is the weather warm in the Carolinas? The temperature is in the mid-seventies here in Miami."

"We're all well. It's a pleasant, sunny day and quite typical for February. Teddy sends his love." Candee paused. "Can I ask you something?"

"Anything, my lovely daughter-in-law."

"What are your views on helping a damsel in distress?"

"Like in the original silent movies where the villain wearing a top hat ties the woman to the railroad tracks? What was that guy's name again?"

"Snidely Whiplash. And no, I mean a beautiful woman needs your help."

"Wait. Who in Roses …" Rob stopped in the middle of his sentence. "I assume you're not referring to yourself."

"Correct."

"Okay then. Who? And why me?" He glanced at his wristwatch. The lunch-hour crowd would be flooding into the bakery soon. Mentally, he estimated the hundreds of cupcakes required to refill the soon-to-be-empty display cases.

"Because you're a professional baker," Candee said. "Plus, you're a perfect gentleman."

"I appreciate the compliments, but where are we going with this conversation?"

"Do you remember my telling you about Kathleen, an Irishwoman from Dublin? She managed The Ground Café."

"Actually, I do," Rob said. "That coffee shop chain recently opened in the States."

"At the time, Kathleen was considering relocating to Roses and starting a teahouse. Well, all that talk became a reality."

Vaguely, he recalled the discussion from a few months earlier. "Congratulations. She made it over the pond okay?"

"Yes, and she's enthusiastic and vivacious and—"

"Good. Wish her luck." He paused to bark instructions to David, a new employee plunging a rack of croissants into a roll-in oven. David had been recommended by a friend of a friend, and Rob had hired him on the spot. High employee turnover and a shortage of staff left him no choice. Too bad the kid hardly looked eighteen, his checkered trousers a size too big for his skinny body, a white torque hat overpowering his small head.

According to his application, David was twenty-something.

Either kids were looking younger, Rob mused, or he was getting older.

"Don't take shortcuts," he directed the newbie. "Check the oven temperature again."

"Yes, Mr. Rob," the newbie acknowledged with a slight bow.

"Do I look like the king of England?" Rob held up a hand, palm up. "Check the temperature, or I'll have you clear out the moat around the bakery."

David gave Rob a blank look and scurried away.

Rob eyed the liqueur. He was inclined to grab the bottle and pour himself a large glass.

Clueless. This next generation was absolutely clueless. Surely the kid realized there was no moat.

The clanging of a pan had him cupping the phone to his ear. "Sorry, Candee. I'd like to chitchat, but it's busier than I anticipated today. Can I call you back tonight? Or better yet, in April."

"Things won't be busy in April?"

"I forgot Easter is in April. Maybe May."

"Isn't Mother's Day in May?"

"June. We'll say June." He ran an irritated hand over his bald head and sighed. "June is the month for weddings. Apparently, a baker's job is never done."

"Coincidentally, Rob, she's a baker too."

"Who?"

"Kathleen. The Irishwoman."

"Right. As we've established, so am I. Tell her cheers, or whatever those Irish people say, and to prepare to never sleep."

"She's lovely."

"Bravo."

"She baked me an Irish brown bread," Candee said. "Her special recipe, and it's delicious."

He slanted over the table to snap off the electric mixer before the over-mixed batter resulted in dense, gummy cupcakes.

"How delicious?" He tried to decide whether he should put the phone on speaker so that he could spoon the batter into tins, or grow a third hand.

"How delicious compared to your cupcakes?" Candee asked.

"Yeah."

"Her bread is the best baked good this side of the Atlantic."

Whoa. Compared to his award-winning cupcakes? Rob frowned and held out a hand to stop an employee from rushing over to him.

"Hold on," he said to Candee. He laid his phone on the counter, yanked off his apron, and stalked to a quiet spot by a window. "Okay, I'm back."

"She is overwhelmed," Candee said. "Relocating to a different country, launching a business from scratch ... I can't imagine how she'll accomplish everything. Do you recall the broken-down diner on Pine Cone Lane? It's been unoccupied for a while."

"The diner is located not far from Keiran's pub, right?"

At his mention of Keiran, Rob rubbed a hand over his eyes. Perhaps he should tell Candee how guilty he felt that he'd been unable to attend the grand re-opening of O'Malley's, the pub Keiran had inherited from his father. Although Keiran and his wife, Desiree, had assured Rob they understood he couldn't leave Miami during the middle of an extensive baking exhibition, he'd missed being in Roses to support them.

"Good memory, Rob," Candee said. "And Kathleen intends to create an old-world teahouse. The problem is the place is screaming for a total remodel. She's experienced, but—"

"What can I do?" Rob conjured up the image of a cherubic, delicate Irishwoman. Slight and fragile, with flaming-red hair and freckles, staring wide-eyed at an undertaking far too large for her.

"You have the expertise and bakery know-how," Candee said.

"Does she need capital and an investor?" Understanding that all new restaurants were under-capitalized, Rob automatically reached for his wallet. A foolish move, he realized, unless cash flew through the phone lines. And even more foolish because he wouldn't see a return on his investment for three to four years.

"She needs advice and support," Candee said. "She's laser-focused on a St. Patrick's Day opening."

"Does she have a business license and sales permit?"

"All set. Fortunately, the diner was already permitted as a restaurant."

"Health and fire department permits?"

"Done."

"Is she making alterations to the building?"

"Major." For the first time, Candee hesitated. "Why?"

He peered out the window. The wrought-iron tables facing his bakery were filled with customers. Between the palm tree border outlining the seating area, low-flowering crepe myrtle trees added pops of vibrant pink blossoms. The effect created a natural arbor, and shade from the bright Florida sun. If customers were comfortable, they tended to stay longer and buy more baked goods.

"She'll need a building permit and possibly a parking permit," he said.

"Good point. I'll check into it."

"Does her business have a name?"

"Kathleen's Teahouse, and the sign is being designed as we speak. She's keeping true to the logo of the old diner. And she's planning to be open ten hours a day and serve break-fast, light lunches, and dinner, as well as tea and baked goods."

"She should add five hours to the beginning and end of

her shift for preparation and clean-up," he said. "Tell her to hire a lot of help, which is forever challenging. Bakery employees find the labor exhausting—both mentally and physically."

"Because of those hot ovens, and they're on their feet so much," Candee commiserated. "Anyway, it's my long-winded way of asking you to come to Roses and give her a hand."

He delayed his response, preparing to launch into a thousand reasons why he couldn't leave his bakeries at such a chaotic time.

"Rob," Candee said, "I know how busy you are."

"You read my mind."

"And I wouldn't phone you if she wasn't in such a bind. The woman is beyond desperate and the place is bleeding money."

Frowning, he strode to the counter and took a sip of the liqueur directly from the bottle. There were plenty of other bottles in the storage room, he rationalized.

"She can email me. No charge for free advice," he said.

Silence on the other end of the phone. Oops. Maybe he'd sounded a little too harsh. A second glance at his watch revealed half past noon. The bakery would be overflowing with people.

He pondered. He hadn't been able to attend the opening of Keiran's pub. However, if he booked a quick trip to Roses, he could be back in Miami by Tuesday.

His bakeries were all closed on Sunday. He'd made the decision since going back to church. It was a religious choice, and a way to honor God.

"You can stay with me and Teddy," Candee pressed. "It will give you an opportunity to see Joseph, the beagles, and Joseph's horse."

The trip made perfect sense. He'd visit with everyone, plus extend his expertise to the Irishwoman. Furthermore,

Roses was absolutely delightful in its slow-paced, countrified way. It would be good to get out of Miami's rat race for three days. Lately, he'd felt exhausted both emotionally and physically.

"Maybe you're right," he murmured.

"Fabulous," Candee said. "You'll love Kathleen. She's all Irish wit and charm. Trust me, you'll want to listen to her brogue all day."

For some reason, Rob felt a little toss of excitement.

Why?

This trip was about a hurried getaway, not meeting an Irishwoman with milky-white skin who brewed perfect cups of tea. She couldn't possibly deal with all that owning a bakery, teahouse, and full-fledged restaurant entailed, so he'd set her straight.

If she was the determined type, she'd remain in Roses, although it was more likely she'd high-tail it back to Ireland before the end of March.

"So when did you say you were arriving?" Candee asked.

"Can Teddy pick me up at the Asheville airport?"

"Absolutely."

Rob took another swig of liqueur. "I'll fly out early Sunday morning, because Saturday is a high-volume day. I'll attend church services on Saturday evening here in Miami."

"Hurray," Candee said with a joyous laugh. "We'll do the same. See you soon."

He started to say more, then stopped, bidding goodbye and clicking off the phone.

How had he been talked into something so quickly?

Truth be told, he was intrigued. This Irishwoman displayed grit by leaving everything behind and coming to America. He guessed she was probably homesick.

He braced a hand on the window sill and stared at the roll-in oven, where smoke was emerging.

"Mr. Rob, do you think the croissants are finished baking?" David, the newbie, asked.

"Did you set the timer?"

"No." David rummaged through a stack of boxes near the oven. "Where is it?

"Do you smell smoke?"

"A little."

"I'd say the entire batch is burned." Rob handed the newbie two oven mitts and snapped a string of instructions. The young man paled and promptly complied, apologizing because it was all his fault.

Rob agreed.

Mitts at the ready, David opened the oven door to a large quantity of burned croissants. He cursed, then swung around. "Are you going to fire me on my first day, Mr. Rob?"

"For cursing?"

"Because … because the croissants are burned."

"I'll give you another chance because I like you."

With that, Rob pushed open the adjoining door to his bustling bakery. Fortunately, no one realized that under his gruff exterior, he was really a marshmallow.

CHAPTER 3

$\mathcal{T}$he following Sunday, Rob stepped off the plane at the modern Asheville airport. He and Teddy exchanged greetings with a clap on the back.

Now that he'd arrived, Rob checked his phone for messages. Although his bakeries weren't open, he oversaw a skeleton crew as they prepared products and ingredients for Monday.

Freeze the stock we selected before you punch out, Rob texted his associate manager.

Roger, his manager replied.

Roger? Really? Who says that? Wasn't the term used for radio communication?

Teddy chuckled, eyeing Rob's exasperated sigh. "I don't miss those days."

"Of slaving over a hot oven? I wish I could say neither do I, but I'm still baking after all these years. Sometimes I wonder if I should sell everything and move to Hawaii."

"Or the Carolinas," Teddy suggested.

"You're always trying to convince me to relocate here."

"I'm simply fulfilling my role as your best friend, and

friends like to be near each other. For camaraderie. And support."

The men had been chums for years. A decade earlier, they'd met at a men's cooking class. Rob had discovered he loved baking and pursued a culinary arts degree. Upon graduation, he'd opened a prosperous bakery chain. Teddy decided he didn't want to be in charge of all that dough (he'd quoted the pun from Julia Child), and, with Rob's capital, became a real estate professional and flipped homes.

After Rob retrieved his luggage, he and Teddy settled into Teddy's pickup truck. Morning sun lightened the sky, and the beauty of North Carolina—from the majestic waterfalls to an old-fashioned swimming hole—brought a sense of relaxation.

"Beautiful state, isn't it? Candee and I love it here," Teddy said.

"Yeah. I may rent a car for an afternoon trip tomorrow."

"You won't be able to explore everything in a few hours, so file it under your list of reasons to move here."

"I don't have a list of reasons," Rob said.

"You should." A grin flashed across Teddy's features. "The other day, Candee read a travel brochure advertising outdoor dining by a pool of water in Asheville. She also cited many art galleries tucked away in little towns within an hour's car ride of Roses."

"Sightseeing it is, then."

"I'd go with you, but I'm tied up with renovating the teahouse, plus helping Candee with her daycare facility. And, needless to say, seeing to Joseph. I assume you'll go by yourself?" Teddy asked.

"Who else?" Rob laughed gruffly. "I can't remember when I last toured anywhere with a companion." He drew down the mirrored sun visor for a quick glance at his reflection, keenly studying the lines of fatigue around his mouth. He was closing in on fifty years old, and the strained creases were showing.

"Frankly, you seem like you need an extended vacation, my friend."

"Uh-huh. Thanks for the advice." Rob flipped up the visor, then smoothed the wrinkles on his Rob's Marvelous Muffins T-shirt. He'd worn the shirt under a navy sport jacket paired with khaki pants. A white cotton square handkerchief showed from his breast jacket pocket.

"I thought my age looked good on me, although I don't see as well as I used to." He chuckled. "Get it?"

Teddy grinned. "I can always count on you for the one-liners. I'm glad you're here. I wish you looked more rested."

Dismissing his fatigue with a wave, Rob replied to a sequence of text messages.

Teddy flicked on the blinker and merged onto the road leading to Roses. "Mind if I ask you a question?"

"Not at all," Rob replied, still absorbed in his text messaging. "I'm perfectly willing to listen. I won't guarantee an answer, though."

"When have you ever actually relaxed?"

Not in forever. Rob didn't share that fact with Teddy, as he'd probably encourage Rob to extend his stay. Although he might be tempted, his bakeries could never operate without him.

"It's high time you enjoyed life," Teddy said. "Worrying about every minute decision will only magnify your problems."

Rob paused, reflecting how best to answer. He switched on the radio to the Bee Gees singing "How Deep Is Your Love".

"Since when have you become so philosophical?" Rob asked.

"A wonderful woman changes a man." Lightly, Teddy

tapped the beat of the song on the steering wheel. "Makes him stop and think about what's truly important."

A ping on his cell-phone drew Rob's attention. His manager asked whether to close an hour later in order to customize a cake for a last-minute wedding.

If you need extra time to get the job done, then sure, Rob texted.

You'll be paying the staff overtime, the manager reminded.

What else is new? With that, Rob snapped his phone shut and jammed it into his pocket. He felt his blood pressure rising. A visit with his physician had confirmed that blood pressure medication would soon be a part of Rob's future. For the time being, he'd refused the brigade of medicines his doctor was all too willing to prescribe.

"That nice-looking Irishwoman might make the ideal companion on your sightseeing excursion," Teddy said. "She hasn't explored the area yet, either."

"Not interested. You and Keiran married the last two good women on the planet."

"There's more than two good women in the world, Rob. And a third is waiting for you to sweep her off her feet."

"Based on the number of my failed dates, a successful match for me is probably somewhere on a remote island in the Pacific. And because I'm not vacationing in the Pacific islands anytime soon, I'd say my dating days are over."

"I don't believe that for a minute." Teddy's expression puckered into a pensive frown, and Rob was reminded of Teddy's older brother, Christian, who had died in a horrific car accident. Teddy had stepped in and gained legal custody of his young nephew, Joseph.

Like his brother, Teddy was dark eyed and tall, and Rob knew Teddy mourned the loss of his brother every day. Teddy and Candee were exemplary parents, raising a child who had been left frail and devastated after the accident.

Fortunately, hours of physical therapy and boundless love had enabled the boy to rebound triumphantly.

"No wonder we never got along," Rob teased. "You're an eternal optimist."

They flew across a bridge, and crushed gravel crackled beneath the truck's tires.

"You'll find your special woman when you least expect it," Teddy said.

Really? Who? He was older now, bald, twenty pounds overweight, and set in his ways. Anyway, bachelor life suited him.

He shifted in his seat. All those long nights in his deluxe Florida condo with a sweeping view of Miami beach had passed in solitude. He filled the void with work, because loneliness only crept up when he had time to think.

He dragged his contemplations away from self-absorption, preferring to stare out the window at the picturesque landscape with a magnificent Blue Ridge mountain backdrop. They traveled past an ancient church, fields of wildflowers, and a garden of violet irises beginning to bloom.

"Candee is preparing a special brunch for us," Teddy said. "Or rather, Keiran is cooking. Desiree hasn't purchased a dining room set yet, so everyone is assembling at my house."

Keiran had met Desiree when he'd been hired to fix up Desiree's Victorian home. They'd married a few months afterward and lived a couple doors down from Candee and Teddy.

"Sounds perfect," Rob said. "I'm always up for a delicious meal."

"Be prepared for pandemonium. Our beagle, Kisses, is full grown. Plus, Candee gifted Keiran and Desiree a pup, and the dog goes everywhere with them."

"The more commotion, the better." Rob slanted his head

back, viewing a row of shuttered buildings. "What town are we in?"

"We're going through Hollan Farms. It's several towns over from Roses."

"Interesting little place." Rob noted mediocre shops and an enormous hotel that dominated the main street. "Someone should give it some TLC. Does anyone live here?"

"At last count there were a few inhabitants. A major factory moved out a while ago, leaving a proverbial ghost town. I heard the entire town is for sale, and the asking price is several million dollars."

Not bad for a place with lots of potential, Rob mused. He was, after all, a businessperson.

A businessperson who could barely handle a half-dozen bakeries in Miami, let alone an entire town.

As they passed through, Teddy indicated the rotted wood on a boarded-up ice cream parlor, then focused a conspiratorial smile on Rob. "Don't even speculate about buying this town to renovate. You have enough on your hands, and should be slowing down to enjoy your wealth."

Rob chuckled. His friend was a mind-reader and knew him like the back of his hand.

"I have absolutely no intention of buying anything," Rob defended brusquely. When skeptical amusement crossed Teddy's face, Rob immediately changed the subject. "How is Keiran's pub?"

"The first few weeks were hectic. At present he's settled in and doing what he loves. Desiree took an extended leave from her law firm to hostess at the pub."

As they entered Roses, Teddy stopped at a crossroads and rounded toward Thompson Lane. The street was lined with trees, large older homes, and plenty of acreage. Window boxes overflowed with velvety purple pansies, ferns, and tulip bulbs, staying true to the traditional origins of the town. Teddy pointed out Keiran and Desiree's Victorian as they drove by.

"Ready to meet Kathleen after brunch?" Teddy eased his truck around the circular driveway and parked in front of his three-story house with its octagonal tower and multi-gabled roof. "Candee has immersed herself in Kathleen's business and vows to make it as popular as Keiran's pub. Too bad the place isn't open yet. Imagine when it is."

"All this Irish charm in one pint-size town," Rob mused. "Sure, I planned on meeting her."

"Excellent." Teddy grinned. "Because she's expecting you."

* * *

THAT AFTERNOON, Kathleen stood on her front stoop and watched a well-dressed bald man wearing a navy sport jacket and khaki pants emerge from Teddy's truck.

Her heart thudded with nervousness. The past few days, endless work had muddled the hours. Today she'd been awake before dawn, baking, attending church, and revising her business plan. She made a mental note to ask Candee if there were any local social media sites where she could advertise.

She'd heard so many stories about the legendary Rob and his marvelous muffins that anticipating his arrival had become an exercise in self-discipline. She flattened the collar of her checkered blouse, critically reviewing her navy-print slacks and sensible leather flats. The mint-green cardigan over her shoulders warded off the midafternoon chill.

She'd half-expected Rob to wear a chef jacket and black trousers, while brandishing a wooden mixing spoon. However, the man confidently striding toward her was solid and broad-shouldered, a warm smile crinkling his face and accentuating his electric-blue eyes. Instead of a wooden spoon, he carried a reflective silver wine bag.

"So you're the lovely Irish rose." He came to the doorstep, stopped within a foot of her, and beamed.

"And you're the famous Rob, who owns bakeries all over Florida."

"Only a half dozen, and they're all located in the Miami area." He grinned. "It saves me from driving all across the state."

"Well, I'll leave you two to get acquainted," Teddy called from his truck. "Rob, when you want a lift back to my place, text me."

"Thanks. Probably in a couple hours." Rob's wave to Teddy was quick before he veered to her. "However, I confess I'm at an impasse."

"A confession already? We just met."

"And an impasse."

She lifted an eyebrow. "Impasse?

"Yes, because I may never want to leave." He extended his hand. "I'm Rob."

"I gathered. Why are you staring at me, Rob?"

"Because you're beautiful, and not at all who I expected."

Near the curb, she heard the purring of Teddy's truck engine.

"Who did you expect?" she asked.

"Not someone who makes me flustered because she's so gorgeous. I get tongue-tied around women like you."

"What?"

"Tongue-tied. At a loss for words."

"For a tongue-tied guy, you're speaking quite well, although I appreciate the compliment." She forced herself to stop and think. "*Was* that a compliment?"

"Absolutely. You remind me of Maureen O'Hara from *Miracle on 34th Street*."

"I love that film. Maureen was originally from Dublin and only twenty-seven years old when she played the role," Kathleen said.

She felt Teddy's gaze on them for another moment before the engine roared and he pulled away from the curb.

"I'm Kathleen, by the way." She accepted Rob's hand. Large and firm, he had the hands of a construction worker with calluses along the base of his fingers. From hours using a rolling pin, she surmised, because she had the same.

"The beautiful Kathleen." He gave a smile, and her heart skipped a beat.

She regarded him, trying to gauge if his words were sincere. She might have given a flippant response, the cool disinterest she employed whenever she suspected men were coming on to her. But wait. Was he—

No, certainly not. Aside from the age difference, he was accomplished and well-educated. She was a country girl who'd grown up in County Galway before moving to Dublin.

He let go of her hand, tugged a bottle out of the bag, and offered it to her. "This is for you. Do you drink Irish liqueur?"

"Tea. I drink tea." She examined the label. "Imported from Ireland?"

"Yes, although this bottle is from Miami. Consider it a housewarming gift. It's a little reminder of your country in case you were homesick."

How did he know she was homesick? A ripple of sadness brought a sting of tears to her eyes that she quickly blinked away.

His gaze fastened on her. "I use the liqueur as an ingredient for a cupcake glaze."

"Thanks."

"I like it," he said.

"Liqueur? Oh, I'm sure." She stuck the bottle in the bag

and set it on the stoop. "Most Irish men love a drink or two."
Or three or four.

"On special occasions?" Rob asked.

"On any occasion. Many were on the lash."

"Meaning?"

"Irish slang for going out drinking." Ruefully, she laughed.
"I've learned to stick with tea, though."

"In that case, so will I." That beam again, flashing
charisma, and firing an attraction inside her that took her
utterly by surprise.

"And I'll teach you how to create the best buttery glaze on
the East Coast," he said.

When, exactly? Candee had told Kathleen that Rob was
only in town until Tuesday. He was a wealthy, successful
man, setting aside a few days from his busy calendar. Most
likely he was overconfident, a tad entitled, and considered
his time more valuable than anyone else's.

"Like you, I'm also pressed for any spare hour these days,"
she said.

"Oh. Sure." He kept his beam. "I understand."

The appeal of his handsome face caused her pulse to leap,
and an awkward heartbeat went by. He waited, apparently,
for her to elaborate about the host of things she had yet
to do.

She didn't respond, just stared at him as if she'd never
seen a man before. She should invite him up to her apartment for tea. However, while she was usually neat as a pin,
the living room and bedroom were in dusty disarray and
boxes were everywhere.

"However, we have a dilemma," he continued.

So do I, she thought. Aloud, she asked, "Which is?"

"How will I prove who is the better baker if we don't bake
together?"

There it was. A not-so-silent gauntlet thrown down between two professional chefs.

Or did he propose more than a bake-off contest?

"We're together now," she pointed out.

"We're not baking. I can show you my cupcake recipe, the one crying out for my celebrated buttery glaze. I presume you store flour and sugar in your apartment's pantry?"

"Of course. I raced to the corner grocer as soon as I arrived in Roses."

"Good." He brought levity to the moment with another smile. "I've heard your Irish brown bread is fabulous."

Aye, they could bake, but she preferred to chat. Here, on her front porch, sitting on the two white wicker rocking chairs Candee had restored, enjoying a cheery afternoon.

Debating, she gazed at the park across the way. February in the South was being pushed to an early spring, and the flower bushes near her entryway displayed the first pink buds. Candee had assured Kathleen that a few more warm days and all the trees would be in bloom.

"Actually, I'm shattered," she said.

His thick eyebrows drew together. They were so close, she saw the threads of gray weaving between the dark hair.

"Exhausted," she explained. "More Irish slang. How about we just chat?"

"I'm up for that." He glanced at his watch, a high-priced brand she instantly recognized. "We can exchange classified information."

"This isn't Scotland Yard," she said. "And my commercial ovens haven't been installed yet, so I've been using the oven in my apartment to bake my breads."

"Will you show me around?"

She felt her cheeks heat. Her apartment? The setting was so intimate.

Aye, that was what he'd asked, and what she'd alluded to. The teahouse seemed the better choice, although kitchen equipment wouldn't begin arriving until Monday. And the large dough mixer was on back order. However, the vendor had assured it would arrive in plenty of time for her grand opening.

She shifted. She was fairly good at thinking on her feet and making quick decisions, but since Rob had arrived, the edges of the afternoon had blurred. Perhaps it was because she enjoyed being with him and hoped to impress him. Woefully, her place was the furthest one got from being impressive.

And he thought *he* was tongue-tied?

She rubbed her hands on her slacks, knowing he stared at her.

"Alright, then. Follow me upstairs," she said. "Before you arrived, I pulled loaves of my Irish breads and batches of scones out of the oven. I'd welcome your truthful opinion on the texture."

Rob seemed the kind of fella a woman could talk to. Despite his affluence, he seemed approachable. Who else wore a T-shirt advertising his company beneath a sport jacket?

She noticed there was no wedding band on the fourth finger of his left hand. Candee had offhandedly remarked he had never married. So he was alone in life, reminding Kathleen of herself.

"Lead the way, my beautiful Kathleen." He stepped nearer. "Have you ever sung, 'I'll Take You Home Again, Kathleen'? It's an Irish ballad."

"The song isn't Irish, Rob." She picked up the gift bag and ushered him around the building. "It has German-American origins."

"I memorized all the words. I'll sing it to you if you'd like."

Before she could answer, he belted out the melody in a

smooth tenor voice, slightly out of tune, warbling lyrics about a wild ocean and a bonnie bride.

She laughed out loud, and it felt good to laugh with a friend, with a man.

Somehow, as they ascended the stairs, she knew she'd always remember this afternoon. The soft, promising breeze on her cheeks, the glint of a dipping sun changing her Carolina world to a silky, golden glow.

And the appealing grin on Rob's features that engaged his entire face. Women could be completely charmed by a man whose emotions were so utterly apparent. He literally wore his sentiments on his sleeve, much like the Irish.

They made their way to the top of the stairs, and he took her free hand as if it were the most natural thing in the world. When they reached the landing, he belted out the second verse, *I'll take you to your home again, Kathleen.*

She joined him, and they sang in unison.

CHAPTER 4

When they reached her apartment, they walked directly into her narrow, cozy kitchen as the screen door banged shut behind them. The floorboards creaked as she hung his jacket on a coat rack in the foyer.

The scent of yeast and sugar flavored the air, and Rob sniffed appreciatively. She invited him to sit at a wooden breakfast nook, consisting of corner unit benches and a table polished in a natural white finish and trimmed in yellow.

"Bread lies at the heart of Irish baking," Kathleen said. Efficiently, she sliced Irish soda bread and went to work on a loaf of brown bread. "Before we eat, let's pray a simple thanks to God." She bowed her head, and he did the same. She whispered a blessing, then offered him a portion of each bread.

The brown bread's crust was thick, the texture dense. The soda bread sprinkled with caraway seed tasted like a biscuit. Although hard on the outside, the inside was moist and delectable.

"Wonderful. I like them both." He helped himself to

another two slices and washed them down with a bottle of water she'd pulled from the fridge.

"The trade secret is cooked raisins." She slid onto the bench across from him. "Save and freeze any leftover raisin water for a later batch. It will produce a sweeter flavor in the bread."

"I like trade secrets." *And he liked her.*

"Brown bread is a well-known Irish staple, so what I'm telling you isn't classified information. This bread is a treasured family recipe from my auntie Peggy."

Rob chewed and bobbed his head, encouraging her to continue.

"Auntie lived twenty days shy of her one hundredth birthday." Kathleen dashed tears from her eyes. "She was slim, walked everywhere all her life, and was witty and fun to be around."

"Do you miss her?" he asked quietly.

"Aye. She used to say that without a slab of brown bread every morning, no Irish kitchen is complete. In fact, you can't go into any pub or bakery without brown bread being on the menu."

"I've never visited Ireland." *Perhaps they could go together.*

"You'd love it." Wistfully, she sighed, although she didn't extend an invitation. "After drinking pints in a pub, this bread has saved my stomach at midnight on many occasions. Topped with a sliver of sharp cheddar cheese and heated in the broiler, it's delicious and not too heavy."

He carved another good sized portion of bread for himself, slathered it with butter, and savored. Awe-inspiring. There were no other words for this woman's baked goods.

"I don't drink, and I'm old enough to admit I've learned a lot through the years," she said. "Giving up alcohol and nights at the pub were two of them. I've witnessed too much heartache. It's been estimated that at least half of all Irish drinkers are problem drinkers."

"Why such a large number?"

"The usual reasons." She looked away. "Affordability, ready availability, and heavy marketing."

"Are you referring to anyone in particular?" Gently cupping her chin in his hand, he directed her to face him.

"My employer, Danny Brady." She eased from Rob's grip, stood and surveyed a decorative ceramic platter in a glass cupboard before reaching for it. "Although not him, because he doesn't drink. His wife, Clara, has a brother who struggles with alcoholism." Kathleen's smoky eyes were remarkably expressive, filled with compassion. "Seamus was a dishwasher for a brief while at The Ground Café. He's been in and out of treatment programs since."

"How is he these days?"

She shrugged casually, a bit too casually considering her shoulders tightened. "Last I heard, he's back in treatment. Success rates for rehab are misleading and aren't as high as people expect."

"If you ever fancy a talk about Ireland, about anything, really, I'm a good listener," Rob said quietly.

"Fancy?" She reached beneath the end bench to a hidden storage unit and retrieved two sage-green place mats. "Is that an American term?"

"I'm trying out your Irish slang."

"*Fancy* is British English." She set the place mats on the table. "And I'll keep your offer in mind."

"Good." He broke the somber mood by gesturing to the counter overflowing with scones. Soon, he'd sampled her blueberry and plain scones baked to a golden-brown, proclaiming them exquisite. As Kathleen directed, he smeared a generous amount of butter and homemade strawberry jam on each.

He grinned. He liked taking directions from her.

Lulled by her lyrical Irish brogue, he listened to her jokes about Ireland's rainy weather and ran his hand down the bench's smooth pine finish. She had a discerning eye for design—it showed in her comfy, appealing kitchen. A leafy English ivy plant hung by the window, a cobalt-blue toaster splashed color on the counter, and a hand-woven rug in a creamy blue weave complemented the tile floor with texture.

"I like your sense of style," he said. "You must enjoy interior decorating."

"Hardly. I find decorating one challenge I prefer to leave to professionals." A smile bloomed on her face. "Tea? I'll put the kettle on."

"Sure."

"You're supposed to say *no, thanks*."

"I am? Why?"

"Because that's what is expected in an Irish home. No worries. We'll try again." Squarely, she faced him. "Tea?"

"No, thanks."

"Brilliant." She grinned, waited a beat. "Tea?"

"What's the correct answer? Yes?"

She pressed her lips needle thin.

"Aye?"

"Have you suddenly become Irish?" she asked.

"No?"

"Third time's a charm. Let's try once more." She smiled. "Tea?"

"Yes. That would be lovely." He folded his hands on his lap and watched her uncertainly.

"Very good."

"Whew." Dramatically, he wiped his brow. "I feel like I almost failed an algebra exam. Should I have started with a *cheerio*?"

"*Cheerio* is another British term and means farewell. Are you leaving?"

"I just arrived." His gaze flicked to the platter of brown bread and he grabbed another slice. "I sought the magic word, and the word *cheerio* always comes to mind when I think of you Brits."

With a heavy sigh, she bent to pick a crumb from the floor. "I'm from Dublin, which is part of the Republic of Ireland. We're our own country and not part of the UK. Shall I enlighten you on the differences between Northern Ireland and the Republic of Ireland?"

He steepled his fingers. "Certainly. I'm quite interested."

"That's a refreshing change. In the States, this topic doesn't often come up."

"I told you I'm an excellent listener." *Good. Excellent. Same difference.*

She seemed to digest his words before she spoke. "Let's get back to our tea discussion, shall we? In Ireland, it's customary to answer *no thanks* twice when offered tea. It's impolite to say *yes* until the third ask." She took a breath. "Once more for practice. Ready?"

He gave a thumbs-up, considered including the word *aye*, but didn't.

"Tea?" she asked.

He held up one finger, then two, mouthing the numbers. "I assume I'm safe because this is at least the third try."

"It's actually the first because we were trying again," she said. "I'll let it pass, though."

"Then I'd love a cup of tea, thank you."

"Cuppa."

"Cup of."

She laughed. "Soon you'll get the hang of it. Are you ready for more questions?"

"Sure."

"Do you prefer milk and sugar? Or a squeeze of lemon?"

"My choice is black tea with lots of sugar." His mouth twitched in amusement as she approved. "I see you Irish take your tea quite seriously," he added.

"Aye, which is why I'd like to teach Americans how to serve a proper tea." She put water in a kettle and placed it on the stove. While waiting for the water to boil, she retrieved two china cups, saucers, and a matching creamer and sugar bowl embellished with blue flowers. She poured milk into the creamer, added lumps of sugar to the open jar, and arranged china and linen napkins on the table.

He considered telling her that if she spent that long preparing each customer's cup of tea, she'd never earn a profit. Instead, he wisely opted for keeping silent as she poured the boiling water into the teapot and their two teacups.

"This warms the pot and our cups," she explained. She waited a minute before discarding the water from the pot and cups into the sink. Then she added two tea bags into the teapot and poured in boiling water.

While he encouraged her to talk about her vision for the teahouse, they filled their plates with more bread. She kept an eye on her wristwatch in between nibbles. After three minutes, she removed the tea bags to an extra plate, stirred the tea, and glided onto the bench.

"First draw?" she asked, preparing to pour.

"I prefer a dark tea."

"Me too." Quickly, she added the tea bags back to the pot for another minute. "A favorite Irish expression is, *strong enough to trot a mouse in* for dark tea."

"Clever. I suggest you not use that expression around your customers, though."

"Mice in the kitchen. The idea would definitely keep patrons away." Her face lightened with wry laughter. "Did you realize the Irish aren't the world's biggest consumer of tea?"

"Who is? England?"

She shook her head. "Turkey, then Ireland, then the UK."

For the next few minutes, he considered voicing his views on buying and selling, and keeping an eye on profit margin. Because he was a competent entrepreneur, he assumed his advice would be welcomed with enthusiasm.

Painstakingly, she poured the tea.

"Thank you." He relished the rich, deep flavor and smiled. They sat silently for a few minutes, savoring their tea.

"If I opened a teahouse," he said, "I'd insert those attention-grabbing tidbits you shared about tea preparation on the menu. Items of interest will enhance your customers' experience and provide them with something to talk about beyond your delectable desserts."

"Maybe." She stared straight ahead while he sipped. Finally, she said, "I'm glad you like tea."

He hadn't said if he liked tea. In fact, he preferred coffee, even over this exquisite brew. But tea was apparently the Irish way, and he sat back on the wooden bench and warmed his fingers around the fragile china cup. Inhaling the fragrant steam, he plated another sliver of brown bread. "Candee was dead-on. Your baked goods are outstanding. And your scones—"

"Thanks. Coming from you, I'm flattered."

"My cupcakes and muffins aren't anywhere near as exciting as your Irish brown bread." He downed the rest of his tea. "I'm thinking about selling fancier pastries in my bakeries. Every one of them needs a face-lift, and foods not normally experienced in standard American shops might benefit sales. Currently, my blueberry muffins are customer favorites. Mind if I pick your brain for innovative European recipes?"

"Certainly. I'm delighted to share what I know." She placed her teacup on her saucer with a clink. "However, if you're turning a grand profit, which I assume you are judging from what Candee has said, why change anything? My ideas aren't any better than yours."

His instinct was to volley her comment back to her while reciting the adage *two heads are better than one*, or some such sage proverb.

However, that wasn't entirely true. The truth was, he wanted to spend time with her, because he could hardly tear his gaze away from her striking face, her delicate smile. She looked utterly gorgeous, her porcelain complexion flushed from a veil of steamy tea.

Mentally, he went over his flight details, suddenly loathe to leave Roses on Tuesday morning. Maybe he'd stay a few extra days, go sightseeing with her, dine with her at the farm-to-table restaurant Candee and Teddy raved about.

"Would you like to see Asheville with me tomorrow afternoon?" he blurted.

"I can't spare the time, although I'm sure Asheville is splendid." Kathleen busied herself with pouring another round of tea. "After March seventeenth, well, perhaps then. Although you don't live here so timing might be difficult."

"I come to Roses often."

"Do you?"

He'd come more now, even if it meant leaving his precious bakeries in the hands of his assistant managers. And to his amazement, he was okay with that.

"By plane, Miami to Asheville is less than a three-hour flight," he said.

"Rob—"

He couldn't gauge her expression beyond that one sharp word. Was she not interested? Preoccupied?

"I'm just saying," he said. "We can exchange phone

109

numbers, alright? In case you need to text me about anything."

"Sure." She gave him her cell-phone number.

He sent her a quick text. *Hi. I'm Rob. 1-800-IRELAND.*

Her smile expanded as she scanned his message. "What does that mean?"

"It means you can call me toll free anytime you need my help and never incur a charge."

She grinned. "I'll remember that. In the meantime—" her voice quieted, seeming to soften her refusal—"I want to stand out with an exceptional product so people will flock to my place. What do you judge to be the best …?"

So she sought his opinion after all, although she'd adeptly sidestepped any personal conversation. When they focused on shop talk, her eyes lit with enthusiasm.

And while they faced each other in her inviting kitchen, he realized something extraordinary. His heart, cold for so long, was thawing. He loved a woman with enthusiasm, and her obvious excitement about her business ignited her smile. He saw the evidence in her dark, gleaming eyes and the way she sat straighter, gesturing with her hands. Her grin widened, displaying white, even teeth. She was already striking. When she elaborated on her innovative concepts, she was altogether alluring.

In turn, she fanned a spark in him he thought had been extinguished long ago.

"… vegan baked goods using organic products," she was saying. "What do you think, Rob?"

What did he think about what? He'd been too preoccupied with gazing at her.

"Rob, were you listening?"

"Of course."

"What did I say?"

"You were mentioning using ground flax meal in your ... scones."

"Aye, that was ten minutes ago."

"People are opting for a wider variety of choices, so consider customers' lifestyle choices when figuring out your menu." He searched his mind for topics he'd discussed with his managers through the years, and added, "Currently, I'm serving carbohydrates, fats, sugar, and caffeine in my shops, so obviously my menus are on the fattening side."

"It's all a balancing act, isn't it?" she asked.

"Life?"

"I was referring to food, but aye, I suppose life too." Pensively, she regarded him, then fished through a kitchen drawer and came back with two sheets of paper and pencils. "How about we combine taste with nutrition?"

We.

"Don't forget your bottom line," he said. "Otherwise, you'll be out of business within six months."

She seemed not to have heard him, intent on her list-making, mouthing the words as she penned them. "Crave-ability," she wrote with a flourish, then pursed her lips. "Is that a word?"

"It is now. And it's a good one."

"Are you interested in going over my business plan with me step by step?" she asked.

"Can I ask you a question first?"

"Aye."

"Have you begun interviewing applicants?"

"No. I'm running an ad in the local paper soon. If I get stuck, Sean, a coworker in Ireland, has offered to assist me."

"How generous," Rob said sardonically.

"He's a dependable manager, and versed in the restaurant business."

"So he's willing to quit his job in Ireland to fly here to help you?"

"Aye."

"There's plenty of suitable workers here in the US." Rob lifted his pencil off the paper. "Should I start listing my ideas?"

"Aye. Fill up the whole sheet."

A thought struck him. Actually two thoughts.

Without admitting it, she'd concurred that two brains were, in fact, better than one. And any comparing of recipes wouldn't be done that evening. He'd already established that anything baked in her oven came out superb.

He tapped his pencil while she wrote an extensive list in a scholarly penmanship he hadn't seen in ages. Nowadays, everyone typed on their computers.

Soon, her list crammed both sides of the paper.

She nibbled the end of her pencil. "This is too much," she murmured. "I'll never complete all these tasks."

"Have you considered prioritizing?" He skimmed the tasks and numbered them according to importance. "And let's pare down this list. You can do that, right?"

"Aye." She consented, humming a familiar Irish folk song, "Oh Danny Boy", under her breath, as she crossed out a word and added alternates.

Hours later, when he gazed through her sheer white kitchen curtains, a full, round moon sailed high in the sky. He glanced at his wristwatch in amazement. The hours spent with her had been nothing short of delightful.

She was a stunningly attractive woman. A woman who touched something powerful and unfamiliar inside him.

Lifting his cell-phone from his pocket, he texted Teddy.

Pick me up at ten, Rob typed.

Did your two hours change to six? came Teddy's reply. *Glad U R enjoying your evening. We were wondering what happened.*

Worried about me?

Always.

I'm fine, Rob typed.

More than fine.

Across the table, Kathleen smiled at him, and Rob's heart did a little meltdown.

Because she's remarkable.

Rob finished his message to Teddy and clicked send.

CHAPTER 5

*A*lthough he tried, Rob couldn't convince Kathleen to play hooky and accompany him to Asheville. She refused, and with good reason considering her opening date of March 17. Instead of sightseeing on his own, he shelved the idea until his next visit, assuring her that he was more than happy to assist her.

While she spent Monday morning securing a line of credit and visiting warehouses, Rob followed breakfasting with Candee and Teddy to lunching at O'Malley's pub, where he assumed head waiter relief for a harried Desiree and Keiran. Pleased the pub appeared busy and profitable, Rob walked the short distance to the teahouse.

Although spring hadn't technically arrived on the calendar, pale lavender crocuses burst through the soil in backyard gardens, and a lazy breeze swept across the grass. Rob plunged his hands into the pockets of his gray windbreaker, delighting in the fresh air against his face. Roses' weather made him feel more animated than he'd felt in ages. February and March were transitional months in Miami, heralding a brief spring before the intense summer heat arrived.

Admittedly, the bounce in his step had more to do with a certain Irishwoman than the temperate weather, his comfortable jeans, or tennis shoes.

As he strolled at a brisk pace, Rob mulled Kathleen's comment from the previous evening.

It's all a balancing act, isn't it?

Yes, he thought. You're so wise. For years, he'd sought to appease thousands of patrons—tweaking recipes, solving every complaint, adhering to the adage "the customer is always right". He'd been so focused on developing his business, he'd pushed aside any notion of personal happiness.

Love? Nope, not even a blip on his radar screen.

Armed with painful past experiences, he struggled to recall why love was so important—why poets wrote sonnets, why it made the world go round.

Because love was everything. Because love mattered above all else.

"Ridiculous notion," he whispered. Besides, he was too old for love. And Kathleen ... well, when he calculated their age difference, he came up with fifteen years.

Had it always been so clear, so straightforward, these unspoken rules for dating and romance? Certainly, problematic circumstances occurred, although Candee encouraged his interest in Kathleen. She'd sensed it immediately, sniffed it out like one of her beloved beagles. In fact, he and Candee had discussed Kathleen throughout breakfast while Teddy looked on with amusement.

Before Rob left, Candee suggested that Kathleen join them for an intimate evening get-together at her home.

"Don't forget to tell Kathleen dinner is at six," Candee reminded as Rob ducked out the door and settled into Teddy's pickup for a ride to town. "And, Rob, a May-December romance is just the thing when two people are so attracted to each other."

He'd given a brief nod, neither agreeing nor disagreeing, although he'd googled age-gap couples on the internet. Studies showed these couples were extremely happy despite social disapproval.

Still, he felt as if his searches let him down, as the findings had encouraged dreams he'd catalogued as unattainable. He wasn't about to fall in love with anyone, including the beautiful Kathleen. Anyone who knew him could recite his unsuccessful dating record. Regardless of his wealth and achievements, women left him flat, and it hurt more than he admitted. No woman chose a man with a retreating hairline (he was being kind to himself—the correct term was bald), and a waistline that increased with every passing year. More important, the sting of heartbreak was too steep an expense for a few weeks of happiness.

WHEN HE ROUNDED the last curve to the teahouse, Rob was out of breath from the final rise in the road. Beneath the overhang of the wide front porch, Kathleen paced impatiently, coming to a stop as if she'd sensed his arrival.

"Hi, Rob." She scratched the back of her neck, her shoulders tight. "I'm relieved you're here."

He puffed to a halt. "Anything wrong?"

"I'm waiting for a distributor to ring me about the oven delivery. I admit I'm terribly impatient. And the large dough mixer is still on back order."

"Sometimes things move slower in the South," he said.

"The same holds true for Ireland." She sighed heavily. "I've been known to snap at people if they're late. I don't want a reputation in the States for being rude. Folks in Ireland accused me of bad behavior on more than one occasion, and I was ashamed and apologized."

"You're a person who likes to get things done. I'm the same way."

Her shoulders relaxed. "Thanks for the assurance."

He caught his breath at the sight of her. That smile. Those deep-brown eyes. He knew he'd think about her every minute of his flight back to Florida. Pausing, he remarked favorably on the exterior of the building, the white glossy trim and exposed brick.

"Teddy's crew is painting the interior and exterior," she said. "He provided a generous bid I couldn't refuse. They started this morning and accomplished a lot already."

"What was his bid? Thousands of dollars?"

"He's offering the labor for free. I'm paying for materials."

"Another reason why I always liked him," Rob joked. He chased ideas across his mind. How could he top Teddy's generosity?

"Please, please come in," she said. The screen door groaned on its hinges as she guided him inside. He envisioned how the diner had been situated—the long counter and various booths were still waiting to be removed. The greasy cooktop hadn't been cleaned in years. On the walls were large black square marks where paintings had once hung.

"The place looks … good," he said. He searched for another word and couldn't find it.

She winced. "Surely, you're joking." She meandered, pointing out wet stains on the ceiling, bemoaning the former owner who had left the windows open, subsequently leading to water damage on the ceiling.

They stepped across the linoleum floor, coated in thick layers of dust.

Amidst the constant pounding of hammers, an Irish band played "When Irish Eyes Are Smiling" on a CD player.

Sounding as if the song had been recorded in a pub, the rousing chorus prompted Rob to sing along.

"You recognize this tune?" she asked.

"Doesn't everyone? Irish music is well-known around the world."

She grinned. "I'm proud to be Irish."

"And I'm proud to know you. You're a resourceful entrepreneur."

"You're a grand fella, just like Candee said."

He chuckled.

"Am I turning scarlet this very minute?" she asked. "For complimenting you?"

They stared at each other in comfortable silence. "A little," he admitted.

She burst into laughter. "Well, that's settled then. Crack on."

"Get to work?"

"Aye."

The blue vinyl seating had been torn out and sat in a heap by the back door. Gingerly, they stepped around it.

"I'm baffled about pricing the scones competitively and hope you can brainstorm with me," she said.

"I'll try, but I should warn you. As I grow older, I'm baffled more often than not."

"About scones?"

"About life in general."

She grinned. "Right, well, welcome to my life too."

She had twisted her strawberry-blond hair into a semblance of a bun, securing the hairdo with pins and a shiny green ribbon. The pulled-back style accentuated her high cheekbones and dainty chin. Her wide eyes seemed too large for her refined features, and the swingy striped T-shirt and baggy sweatpants reflected her commitment to hard work, not to being a slave to the latest fashion.

Once at an empty booth, Kathleen plunged into ordering kitchen equipment, leaving little time for chitchat save for her sharp questions. He pulled off his windbreaker, rolled up his sleeves, and sat across from her.

"Tea?" she finally asked.

"Oh no. Will it be an all-day process?"

"Only a few minutes, I promise. And I'll take your answer as an *aye*." She climbed the interior steps to her apartment and came back carrying a tray chock full of stoneware—cups, a teapot filled with steaming tea, sugar and creamer, and scones from the previous evening.

Today she wasn't glamorous. Today she was simply breathtaking. Despite her flushed cheeks, her complexion was bone-white, revealing dark shadows under her eyes. Bound by the invisible strands of a strong work ethic, he'd later look back on the afternoon as the best he'd spent in decades.

In between her visiting with suppliers who stopped in and a meeting with a service rep, he inquired about her years as head assistant for Danny Brady. He even pressed for information about her dating past, to be sure no man waited for her in Ireland.

Her responses were vague, although she revealed she'd dated a couple fellas and discovered both were liars. Actually, she used the word *eejit*.

"These days, I'm embarrassed I was a stook for believing them," she said.

"*Stook* is another Irish word for idiot?"

"Aye." She wove her fingers together and glanced at the floor.

By late afternoon one of the ovens had been delivered, and the last of Teddy's crew packed his tools and left. She stepped over to a rusty sink to wash her hands for the umpteenth time, and Rob came beside her.

"I'm leaving tomorrow," he reminded. "I hope you'll join me for dinner tonight at Candee and Teddy's house."

She wrenched the faucet shut. "Is that an invite?"

"A sincere invite."

"I'm sorry." Her expression became pensive. "I wish, but I'm drowning here."

"I'm wishing too." He wished he could stay in Roses. Another day, another two days. She hadn't encouraged him, although he'd dropped several broad hints.

He decided to take matters into his own hands. He couldn't help himself.

Gently, he brought her to face him. Before she could reply, he bent his head and kissed her, a feather-light touch of his lips to hers.

She tasted of tea and sugar, her fragrance the subtle scent of lavender.

At first, she didn't move. When his hand curved around her back and the kiss deepened, she broke free.

"Obviously," she said, "we're not going to start dating."

"Why?"

"Because you live in Miami. And I live in Ire … I mean, Roses."

"That's why they invented airplanes. And cell-phones."

She moved backward. "You, of all people, should know I'm not interested, given you've heard my dating history."

"So you dated a few guys who were rogues. Not all of us are like that."

"*Rogue* is a harsh word." Her reddish-brown eyebrows lifted. "Is the term American?"

"I've never used the word before. I assumed it was British, and I was trying to impress you."

"Irish. I'm Irish." She gazed at him and her smile came slow, lighting her heart-shaped face. She was delightful—part cherub and part tigress. His heart beat in double-time.

"My dating track record wouldn't win any awards, either," he said quietly.

She studied him.

Fearful she might feel sorry for him, an old guy, a desperate bachelor, he waved a hand indifferently. "I'm only telling you so we can commiserate."

"About love and romance?"

"About commonality. We both target accomplishment above all else."

"From the sounds of it, we're both workaholics."

The quiet lasted several beats, punctuated only by the drip, drip, drip of a tarnished faucet.

"You know, I could use someone like you in my bakeries," he said. "Someone energetic and organized."

"*Your* bakeries?" Her Irish brogue thickened. "In Miami?"

"Yes. You'd like Miami. It's—" He'd been about to say it was hot and humid before stopping himself. He certainly couldn't illustrate a Miami travel brochure if those were the only adjectives coming to mind.

She plunked her fists on her hips. "As you are certainly aware, I have my own business right here in Roses."

"How could I forget?" He tugged on his windbreaker. "We've dreamt up a million ideas about it all afternoon."

"Don't you understand? I need to do this on my own."

"I understand that you won't allow me to help you."

"By giving everything up? Why would you ask me such a question?"

Because he didn't want to leave her. And he couldn't just abandon his businesses. Hers was just starting up. Perhaps she could sell the diner. Or the teahouse. Or whatever she preferred to call it.

Thankfully, he kept his opinions to himself, for when he rotated, he confronted narrowed eyes and a stormy expression.

"You'd learn a lot," he said, "and I'd promote you to a manager in my flagship Miami bakery."

"Surely, you're joking. *Flagship* was my middle name in Dublin. Been there, done that."

"You won't earn a decent salary here for months, maybe even years."

Definitely the wrong thing to say, judging by the anger flashing from her dark eyes.

"Haven't you heard a word in all the hours we've spent together? My answer is no. Absolutely not." She spun and gathered up the stoneware, placing cups and teapot on the tray.

"What about this evening's invite?" he asked. "Candee and Teddy are expecting us."

"Tell them I'll probably see them tomorrow." She picked up the tray. "You may not live in Roses, Rob, but I do."

"I can stick around a few more hours. Really. I'll text Teddy and—"

"No. We're done here." Resolutely, she shook her head. "Enjoy the flight back to Miami and thanks for your help."

CHAPTER 6

The following morning, Kathleen was awakened by persistent hammering coming from the floor below her apartment. The sun poured into her bedroom window and she checked the time, knowing she'd overslept.

After a quick shower, she gulped some tea and hastened downstairs.

The five crewmen who greeted her caused her to stop short. All the scene needed was a foreman. As the word came to mind, Teddy appeared. In a lazy southern drawl, he adeptly guided the men to sheetrock, sand and paint. As he joked with them, she could hardly believe he ran such a large construction firm, because he was so laid-back.

Of course, the same held true for Rob. His winning smile was disarming, and he'd been heralded as Miami's most successful entrepreneur.

His dry humor was comfortable, cheerful, and concise. After he'd abruptly left the day before, her reflections continued to revolve around him. Not her business plan, nor her scones, nor a proper cuppa. Just him.

"Good morning, Kathleen." Candee waved from the

doorway of the back room. "Teddy and I came to see how your place is progressing."

Kathleen sucked in her bottom lip. "Good as gold, thanks to Teddy."

"It's a virtual circus around here, but a good sign because it means things are moving quickly."

"Aye." Kathleen fidgeted with the skirt of the apron she'd thrown over her jeans and charcoal-gray sweatshirt. She knew she looked a sight and slanted a glance toward the workers. By way of an explanation, she said, "I was experimenting with a new recipe for scones last night, and went to bed later than I planned."

"You're worn out."

"Knackered is the Irish word."

"Have you eaten breakfast?"

"Black tea."

Candee waved several brown bags in the air. "You must eat a decent meal or you'll fade away. Teddy and I brought you a typical southern breakfast, but I won't take credit for the cooking. Grits and eggs, buttermilk biscuits and sausage swimming in creamy white gravy, compliments of Keiran."

"Thank you. I haven't had the chance to meet him yet."

"As you're aware, he has family in Dublin so you'll have lots to chat about." Candee flashed a sunny grin. "C'mon. Let's eat."

"I won't be able to fit into any of my clothes," Kathleen warned, while Candee led her through the back room, littered with debris. By the window facing the yard, they assembled at a three-legged table salvaged from the diner. A chest of drawers Kathleen had brought from Ireland held some of her personal belongings.

Candee brought out warm food wrapped in foil containers, complete with silverware and cloth napkins. For herself, she set carry-out coffee and sugar packets on the table.

"I assume you drink tea," Candee said as she poured three packets of sugar into her coffee and stirred.

"I've had my fill for now." Kathleen pulled a bottled water from the cooler.

She perched at the end of the booth, gestured for Candee to sit across from her, and said a blessing. Although she'd baked, she hadn't prepared a proper meal for herself since she'd arrived.

"I'm sorry you weren't able to join us last night," Candee said over the rim of her coffee cup.

Kathleen helped herself to another forkful of eggs. Candee had bragged about Keiran's cooking with obvious good reason.

"I'm hoping for a raincheck," she said. "I'd love to see your home."

"Rob missed you."

Kathleen felt her cheeks color. "We had a slight disagreement."

"He was unusually quiet at dinner."

Thinking over his offer tugged hard on Kathleen's mood, and she took a deep breath. "He assumed I'd prefer to work for him rather than run my own business."

"He said that?"

"He suggested I become a manager at his bakery in Miami. Why on earth would—?" Kathleen broke off.

"Only one reason."

"Which is?" After studying Candee's determined features, Kathleen sensed the answer. "You think this was his way of us being together?"

"Are you ... together?"

"We met a few days ago. Surely you don't believe we're falling in love."

With a bemused smile, Candee said, "Why do you think people call it falling in love? Love develops quickly and feels like you're losing control. You know—falling, tripping—"

Kathleen dismissed this with a head shake. "I'm not seeking any type of courtship. Too often, I've failed in the dating department. I'm good at business. Strictly business."

She wasn't an obsessed, clingy woman who needed a man. At least, not anymore.

Nonchalantly, Candee sipped her coffee. "Every person is different. You'll know when the right man comes along."

Like Rob, for instance?

No. Not happening.

Blankly, Kathleen stared at the paneled wall behind Candee. Admittedly, thoughts of Rob consumed her. He made her feel relaxed and encouraged, telling her she could handle the most difficult situation. And he'd made it clear he was available.

She heaved a breath. At this rate, she was focusing more hours and energy on him than her teahouse. How would she ever create a tea emporium if she couldn't even manage to get menus finalized?

"Why don't men ever listen to women?" she asked.

"Because men and women are wired differently," Candee replied. "Knowing Rob, he was only trying to help. He doesn't understand why you should struggle when he can do so much for you."

"He said that?"

"Yes."

"I know he believes in me," Kathleen said. "Now I want him to stand back so I can face the challenges on my own."

"He's a man who looks at a problem and presents a solution. He's practical. Once you learn more about him, you'll understand."

Oh, but she had learned about him. Beneath their light bantering she'd discovered he'd never married and wasn't currently dating. Beneath his laughter, she felt certain he'd been hurt. On their first night, he'd revealed his home life had been filled with rejection. His parents had never responded favorably to his bids for affection and hadn't approved of his profession.

There was more. She knew there was more, although he hadn't spoken of it. Perhaps someday. At present, she wouldn't push, wouldn't pry. Besides, when would she see him again?

Beneath his commanding exterior she sensed an easily bruised sensitivity. And with that insight, she was more attracted to him. Because he was vulnerable, just like her. Sometimes the most prosperous men were the most insecure. Perhaps it was the reason why he was driven to succeed.

She stared out the window. Sunlight exposed floating dust particles. A fluorescent light bulb buzzed overhead, calling attention to the discolored ceiling.

"The thing is," Kathleen said, "Rob is fun to be around. He's well-educated and freely shares his experience."

"When Teddy needed a friend, Rob was there. He's loyal and generous." At Kathleen's inquisitive expression, Candee added, "The next time he comes to Roses, you might see his generosity in action. He's involved in several charitable organizations, including one with Keiran."

"Rob comes to Roses often?"

Candee grinned. "He will now."

Kathleen's heart swelled. When Rob had smiled at her, kissed her, she'd felt a shiny spin of hope. Perhaps here, in America …

No. She refused to dwell on a future that could never be. If she and Rob dated, she knew the ending. Men left her without a care. Every single time.

She concentrated on the last of her biscuit and white

gravy. Some people were meant to live life alone. She was one of them.

"And do you know why?" Candee asked.

"Know why what?" Kathleen glanced up, noting Candee's mischievous grin. "Why Rob will be back? Do you know something I don't?"

"Me?" Candee feigned an expression so innocent, Kathleen burst out laughing. "He talked about you the entire evening and kept looking at his phone," Candee went on. "I think he was hoping you'd reconsidered our invite."

"I couldn't." Kathleen stood and threw open the window to let in some fresh air. "Look around."

"You sent him back to Miami with your rejection." Accusation colored Candee's voice.

Kathleen bristled. "Wasn't he leaving, anyway? He owns a half-dozen bakeries."

"He wanted to stay longer. In fact, he'd been in touch with his Miami assistant manager."

Kathleen knew her cheeks colored. Aye, her refusal had been blunt, but she'd worked for others her entire life. Wasn't sacrificing all those sweat-filled years enough?

"I didn't mean to hurt his feelings, although I doubt he was affected," she said.

"Did you apologize?"

"What?" Kathleen's eyes widened. "He should apologize to me."

Candee settled her elbows on the table and rested her chin on her fists. "Have you heard from him?"

"He texted me last night." Again, Kathleen stared out the window at the post-card perfect sky.

The previous afternoon, she and Rob had tossed designs around. Their conversation had been easy, and she hadn't laughed so hard in years. She'd been impressed with his quick mind, the ease in which he'd presented practical, timely solutions to her questions, writing extensive lists with his bold left-handed scrawl.

"What did he say in his texts?" Candee asked.

"He said he enjoyed his time with me. I wished him a safe flight," Kathleen said.

"Unfortunately, you're both too polite."

Kathleen took note of Candee's set jaw. "Meaning?"

"You didn't discuss what really matters."

"Dating?" Kathleen clenched her hands together. "When I'm drowning in business loan debt?"

"Love is the only thing that matters."

"Maybe in your world. Certainly not in mine. What matters is that I'm starting a brand-new venture and can't concentrate on anything else."

Candee doctored her coffee with another packet of sugar and took a long swallow. "I admit Rob is a little high-handed at times."

"It's because he's skilled and on the ball. And funny and warm-hearted."

Exactly what the other men in her life had lacked. In the short days they'd known each other, Rob had displayed a tenderness she hadn't noticed at first, developing in the course of their hours together. She'd listened as he'd laughingly remarked about his dismal dating history. Although he'd airily portrayed himself as a man who couldn't care less, his admission seemed more heartbreaking than humorous.

"Wow, Kathleen." Candee set down her cup. "You're quick to come to his defense."

"I—" Kathleen rubbed her palms on her sweatshirt.

"I see you're interested in him. It's written all over your face. Admit it."

Kathleen averted her eyes from Candee's attentive gaze. Despite her exhaustion, she hadn't slept well. If she had more time, she might have talked further about Rob, but the sentences wedged in her throat. Unfortunately, time was something she lacked, and life went on.

She walked back to the table and dabbed her lips with her napkin. "What interests me is designing this blank space into a charming teahouse in a few short weeks." As she disposed of the containers, Candee wrapped the silverware and napkins.

Through the doorway, Teddy and his crew set up ladders, arranged tools and prepared joint compound.

Kathleen perused the bare walls. She'd never considered interior decorating her strong suit despite Rob's compliments. In any case, he'd only seen her kitchen.

"How can I best utilize every inch of space?" she asked aloud.

"This is where I come in." Candee popped to her feet.

For the next several hours, Candee shared design tips while drawing up a floor plan, adding extra windows and laying out a well-equipped kitchen complete with sinks, a cooler, and oven placement. When Kathleen peered over Candee's shoulder, Candee said, "No worries. I'm keeping in mind the strict health code."

Meanwhile, Kathleen grabbed scrubbing supplies and tackled the shelving.

When they finished, Candee locked arms with Kathleen and yanked her out the front door. "And now, we're going shopping."

"My pantry is stocked with flour and baking soda."

"Good, because we're canvassing all the paint stores for samples. Fun bright colors will look terrific on the interior walls, and I suggest leaving the exposed brick behind the counter. Build a fireplace on the far wall with a wide pine mantel."

"Let's section the rooms to keep them more intimate," Kathleen said. "The smaller room can seat ten to twelve people, the larger up to twenty. I want worn leather couches in the sitting area, a loveseat, and blackboard by the entrance so I can chalk in the soups of the day." A wave of excitement coursed through her as more ideas took hold. "Creamy broccoli or parsnips with apple and curry are favorite soups in Ireland."

"Parsnips?" Candee asked. "What are those?"

"A root vegetable similar to a carrot, only cream-colored."

"When parsnip soup is on your menu, call me," Candee said. "Now, over and above food, let's get back to decorating. Stripping the wood on the sideboards will create an antique feel."

"At some point, I'll need a taste tester for the scones and bread."

Candee paused. "Is that all you think about—food?"

"I own a teahouse, not a bookstore."

Candee gazed at her with an overly satisfied expression. "I know the ideal person for the job."

"Who?"

"Rob."

Kathleen's pulse skipped a beat. The subject, the man she'd avoided talking about all afternoon, brought a smile she couldn't contain.

"Aye," she agreed.

Did her enthusiasm make her look transparent? The twinkle in Candee's eyes gave Kathleen her answer.

Aye.

CHAPTER 7

*R*ob stood in the backyard of Candee and Teddy's Victorian mansion, gazing at the enclosed pasture. Teddy had converted a large shed into a stable and purchased a Haflinger horse, sturdy and energetic with a flaxen mane, for Joseph's therapy.

When Joseph got off the school bus, Rob was propped against the fence admiring the home's gingerbread trim, which Candee had painted burnt-sienna. The shade nicely offset the mustard color exterior.

"Mr. Rob!" Joseph squealed in delight as he charged down the driveway. "I'm so happy you're back in Roses!" Out of breath, he dropped his bookbag on the ground and launched into Rob's arms. "How long will you stay?"

Rob managed a jovial smile. "A few days, maybe more."

Maybe less. It all depended on how a certain beautiful Irishwoman responded when he showed up at her teahouse.

After Candee had phoned him, breathless with the news that Kathleen had spoken favorably about him, she'd used her finest singsong voice and urged him to return to Roses.

That took some planning, but he'd assembled his managers and arranged the necessary details.

"I'm only a phone call away," he'd assured, with the unspoken hope no one rang.

So here he was, a week later, back in Roses. This time, he vowed not to talk shop with Kathleen. At least, not *his* shop. He was here merely to lend a hand.

As the opening drew nearer, she might fly into a panic. Consequently, he was ready and able to offer his support.

"Mr. Rob, what do you think of my horse?" Joseph tipped his head toward the small horse being led out of the stable by the therapist.

"I think your horse is awesomely pint-sized," Rob said.

"His name is Blackjack," Joseph said with an impish smile.

Nearing seven years old, the little boy had quickly emerged from a preschooler to a thriving second grader. The freckles on his cheeks were disappearing and baby teeth had begun to fall out, leaving a gap-toothed grin.

"Yes, I know. Even though Blackjack is chestnut colored and not at all black."

"Blackjack doesn't mind." Joseph's face shone with happiness. "He likes his name."

Rob touched the boy's chin. "I'm sure he does."

Teddy and Candee's love and affection had strengthened the boy's self-esteem, and he bore little resemblance to the broken child Rob remembered from a few years earlier.

"Rob?" Teddy called from the back porch. "Are you ready? Kathleen's expecting you." Thumbs hooked in his front jean pockets, he grinned indulgently. Whenever he spoke to Rob about Kathleen, he smirked. Just like Candee did.

"Be right there," Rob said.

"I've gotta go too, Mr. Rob." With a breeze tangling his fine hair and an eager smile on his face, Joseph scampered away.

A few minutes later, Rob arrived at the teahouse. In several days, the exterior had been transformed from drab to grand. The old-world appearance Kathleen strived for conveyed a welcoming invitation to passersby. Her signage, Kathleen's Teahouse, stained in lavender and blues and exaggerated by pink teacups, had been fixed high above the entrance.

His gaze roamed enthusiastically over the renovated building. Afternoon had settled, and the windows were aglow with lit electric candles.

A very welcoming place indeed. He just hoped the owner's heart held the same welcome.

WATCHING THROUGH LOWERED LASHES, Kathleen stood on her front porch as Rob got out of Teddy's pickup and waved a thanks. The work crew had retired for the day and the house was empty. They began at seven in the morning and clocked out at three thirty, so without the constant rat-a-tat-tat of hammering, the hollowness echoing through the rooms was oppressive.

"Cheers," she greeted Rob as he approached. "It's good to see you."

"A greeting from a beautiful woman is the best form of welcome," he said.

She smiled. "The Irish are known for their hospitality." As much as she tried, she couldn't tamp down the flurry in her chest at seeing him again.

Should they embrace like great friends, erasing their silly squabble? He had texted an apology and she'd done the same. Since then, the subject of her moving to Miami hadn't been broached. Thankfully, that had been settled.

She kept her hands at her sides while considering what to do next.

"It's good to see you again too." His blue eyes were steady and genial, startlingly intense. His tan golf shirt fit his frame perfectly, and he carried himself as a self-assured man, not a young guy who'd disguised his identity on the internet. Rob's tastes were sophisticated, and he was cultured and witty, an enticing combination.

No doubt about it. No matter how she resisted, she was drawn to him.

An expression of unconcealed admiration touched his handsome face. "I came back for you."

"Because of me, or for me?"

"Both."

"Did you assume I needed help, or did you want to see me?"

"Both."

"So you're not here to sightsee or visit friends?"

"I'm here exclusively for you." Warmly, he appraised her. "And you look gorgeous."

"Gorgeous? Hardly." Self-consciously, she patted her hair and offered a fatigued smile. Then she tugged at the pinstriped blouse and dark-washed jeans she'd changed into after a quick shower. Rob had texted saying when he'd arrive, but, as usual, she hadn't allowed enough time for herself and had settled for braiding her hair and applying pink lip gloss.

"Kathleen." He stepped closer. "I missed you. And I want you to know how much."

"You've only been gone a short while."

"The days were long for me."

The heat in her cheeks became a full-blown fire. Her gaze dropped to the flowers he held.

"I missed you too," she said quietly.

Attraction was a funny thing. It made you forget about feigning disinterest, a game suited for years thankfully well past.

"These are for you." He offered the flowers. "I asked the florist in town for something Irish."

"They're lovely." Kathleen accepted the bouquet of fresh-cut green and white button mums and carnations, the perfumed fragrance reminding her of the bushy plants growing wild in County Galway.

Her beloved Ireland. Nostalgia rushed through her, clogging her throat with emotion.

"Thank you," she managed.

"Are you homesick?"

"A little, although it's childish." Her eyes turned liquid, and a tear streaked down her cheek. "This is what I wanted—America and my own business. Fortunately, I've kept myself so busy my mind doesn't have time to wander."

Gently, he brushed the tear away. "I'm here and not going anywhere. Teddy and Candee said I can stay at their house as long as I'd like."

"What about your bakeries?"

"My marvelous muffins are so marvelous they practically bake themselves."

Despite herself, she chuckled.

He took the flowers from her, set them on the porch's wide railing, and gathered her into his arms.

She'd dreamt of this moment ever since they'd parted, and she didn't resist. Instead, she pressed her cheek along the smooth cotton of his shirt. The steady beating of his heart reassured her that he was here, truly here. And all was well.

He'd texted and emailed nightly since her talk with Candee. Which, he'd admitted, had prompted his return.

His emails were humorous and engaging, often describing a nonsensical situation occurring at work—a customer demanding a slice of huckleberry pie, although his bakery clearly sold only muffins and cupcakes and croissants, or an experimental batch of seaweed muffins everyone refused to eat.

We try to sell healthy selections once in a while, he'd joked.

What did you do with all those wholesome muffins? she'd asked.

I gave them to my skinny employees. Along with the remaining seaweed.

Oftentimes, his solutions to her work-related questions were exceptional. And when she uploaded photos of the daily progress to share with him, he replied instantly. Nothing was too unsettling that Rob couldn't solve with a clever, sensible remedy.

Each evening, when she was too exhausted to decide on another scone recipe or the installation of a gas versus a wood-burning fireplace, she looked forward to the end of her workday. She could finally climb the stairs to her apartment, open her laptop, and eagerly read his email.

When worries about money kept her awake at night, Rob would message her as soon as she logged onto her computer, as if he'd waited up for her. Sometimes, his messages were flirtatious. The actuality that he was eight hundred miles away made their exchanges feel safe and risk-free, and she enjoyed the playful bantering.

"The place looks better in person than in your photos," Rob said as she plucked up the bouquet and they stepped inside. He beamed his approval, sniffing the cedar-scented air and indicating the blazing logs in the stone-faced fireplace. "You decided on wood instead of gas after all."

"Aye." She went to the sink, retrieved a crystal vase, and arranged the flowers. "It's more work, but wood-burning is more authentic. And Teddy's hard-working crew deserves the credit, along with Candee's decorating expertise."

"I love these photographs." He stepped to a white-washed

wall and surveyed the black and white photos of the old diner.

"I chose to pay homage to the diner's legacy. This place is riddled in history and was originally named Betty's Diner."

She'd set a table in Victorian style, complete with an Irish lace tablecloth, bone china cups, and polished silver. She set the vase of flowers in the center.

"Do you like the ambience?" she asked, following his reaction.

"Very, very much." He lifted back a pale-blue wool Oriental rug. "The wide plank oak floors are gleaming and rustic, which was the effect you were going for, right?"

"Absolutely." She tipped up her chin. "The crystal chandeliers will be hung tomorrow. And the paintings depict Ireland's landscapes. I placed them on the wall opposite the photographs, highlighting the old and the new, and two different cultures." She indicated a particularly poignant watercolor of a stone castle atop a hill, the rugged coastline and sea beyond. "I borrowed this concept from Danny Brady. Irish murals grace the walls in The Ground Café."

Rob came beside her. "Kathleen, you are a treasure." His sincere smile melted her heart. He bent his head and kissed her temple, then brushed a butterfly kiss on her lips. Joy surged through her that had nothing to do with his compliment. She couldn't believe this delightful man was interested in her.

And he was. It showed in his avid gaze, his steady eye contact and how he engaged her in endless chats.

"Would you prefer high tea or afternoon tea?" she asked.

"What's the difference?"

She glanced at her wristwatch. "It's around four, so afternoon tea is better."

"Again, what's the difference?"

"Mostly the seating. Afternoon tea is best experienced on low parlor chairs. If it's a high-backed chair, then it's high tea."

"Easy facts to remember," he said. "So these are low chairs."

"Correct."

"Is there a story behind high and low tea you can place on your menus?"

"I'll give you the abridged edition if you're interested."

"If it concerns you, I'm very interested."

"Well, teatime is a British tradition." She steepled her fingers. "Customarily, tea, scones, cakes and sandwiches were served in the nineteenth century. Teatime filled the gap between lunch and dinner, which was usually eaten around eight o'clock."

"I eat muffins every day at four. Should I call my snacks teatime?"

"If you'd like." She chuckled. "Nowadays, obviously, routines have changed. However, teatime is still observed as a civilized tradition. More important, it brings friends and family together and allows everyone the chance to slow down."

His eyes crinkled into a smile. "I'm more than ready to slow down."

Aye, she reasoned, noting the low crease in his forehead. Despite his smile, he looked as exhausted as she felt.

She whisked a glance at a log dropping in the fireplace. The wood sparked and crackled. Knowing his gaze was on her, she donned her prettiest beam. "So, shall we enjoy afternoon tea?"

"Sure. I think."

She laughed out loud at his wary expression. "You think?"

"Mind briefing me on what afternoon tea entails? I

understand the four o'clock part, but is this another no thank you three times discussion?"

"We've done all that." She gestured for him to sit in a flowered parlor chair at the intimate table set for two.

He didn't.

Instead, he pulled out a chair for her before claiming his own. He was a gentleman in numerous ways, opening doors for her, never sitting if she was standing. Always, he was respectful and polite.

She poured the hot tea, which she'd prepared ahead. Gold flatware glinted by the light of tea candles, and metallic gold linen napkins folded in the shape of a crown sat on bone-china plates, the plates so translucent as to be almost see-through. A tiered platter was set with scones, finger sand-wiches, clotted cream, and strawberry preserves.

"Is your tea dark enough?" she inquired.

He made a show of examining the brew in his gold-rimmed cup. "Strong enough to trot a mouse in."

"Here, here." She chuckled. "You're learning the Irish sayings quickly."

They bowed their heads and prayed a blessing. When they finished, she presented turkey sandwiches covered in cranberry jelly from the platter.

"I could get used to this," he laughed, taking a bite of a cucumber finger sandwich spread with herbed cream. "How did you make the cream?" he asked.

"It's not difficult. I'll lend you the recipe."

He settled in, slid his teacup closer, and supported his elbows on the table. Tea sloshed over the rim of his cup. "Kathleen, you've made the entire process look easy. You're going to open without a hitch."

The table wobbled, the legs uneven. And with that, the exquisite settings, hot tea, sandwiches, and flower-filled vase clattered to the floor.

Kathleen caught her teacup between her palms, although the brew spilled across her pinstriped blouse, leaving behind a splotchy wet stain. She dabbed at her shirt, her fingertips catching the droplets.

"Aye," she echoed, perching on the edge of her chair. "I'll be opening without a hitch."

CHAPTER 8

To his customers and everyone in Miami who presumed to know him, Rob's bakeries were the epitome of success. To Rob, his bakeries were fast becoming a weight too heavy to carry on his broad shoulders.

And he was seriously considering selling everything.

More and more, Miami had become a place he sought to escape. He was tired of setting aside his personal life for an ever-elusive joy, no matter the vast amount of wealth and accolades he'd accumulated.

He craved laughter and companionship with people he enjoyed.

With Kathleen.

However, he also wanted to make certain their bond was more than a casual exchange between two businesspeople.

The following afternoon, he sat in the back room of Kathleen's teahouse with his cell-phone on speaker. George, his manager, was working in the Miami office, and he'd asked David, the newbie, to be his messenger and relay the bad news to Rob.

Butter prices had substantially risen and were up by 75 percent.

"Tell George to shop around," Rob told David.

"He has, Mr. Rob," David said. "All the local vendors and bulk supply stores have increased their prices."

"Their timing is perfect for the spring baking season. That is, perfect for them," Rob said sardonically. "I'll recalculate our muffin prices so we can stay within profit margins."

"Not possible, sir, unless you're planning to charge five dollars per muffin," David said. "We're currently selling at two dollars apiece."

"And losing money," Rob pointed out. "Although no customer will buy a five-dollar muffin, no matter how marvelous."

"Correct, sir."

"I'm proud of my products. However, I'm not in business to give them away." Impatience thickened Rob's tone. "Tell him."

"Yes, sir." David muffled the phone, and returned a minute later. "George said he's well aware of that, sir."

Heaving a sigh, Rob tipped his head against the back of the chair.

"Rob?" After a light tap on the door, Kathleen's voice floated through the room. "Oh, sorry." She put a hand to her mouth in apology. "I didn't realize you were still on the phone."

The afternoon sun shone through the window, splashing her cheeks with a hint of color. The past three days, she'd worked nonstop from early morning to late evening. Between Teddy's crew and a constant stream of suppliers, organized commotion heralded each new day. Rob had appeared each morning at daybreak, rolled up his sleeves, and worked alongside her.

He smiled at her, stood, and held up an index finger to let her know he was finishing the call.

"Text me later with a better update," he said to David. "Or we'll be churning our own butter."

"No worries. We'll need a cow, though, sir."

Rob stared at his cell-phone in stunned disbelief.

Apparently waiting for a response, David stacked on more assurances. "Actually ... we'll probably need two cows, sir."

Frustration reduced Rob's response to a groan. When he did speak, he kept his tone purposefully calm. "Thanks for the helpful tip, David. Goodbye for now." He clicked his phone shut and tossed it across the table.

Kathleen's lips twitched, a twinkle in her sparkling eyes. "You're in the business of buying cows now, are you? I'll take a half dozen. I heard Candee and Teddy own a pasture."

He laughed heartily. With her, every minute was like being in the middle of a splendid dream. She had an aura of exhilaration, a freshness sparking something inside him. Most important, she let him forget his cares, at least for a while.

Strawberry-blond tendrils had worked loose from her high ponytail, which she'd tied back with a teal satin ribbon. She wore a stretchy-knit yellow dress with a pretty V-neck-line and tan loafers.

He'd dated beautiful women in his lifetime. No one compared to Kathleen. Perhaps it was her porcelain complexion, or the figure-hugging dress showing off her curves, or her shiny hair glinting in the sunlight. Perhaps it was because, besides being downright striking, she was chic and confident.

And yet she had never married. What was going on in Ireland? Were all the men blind?

Grinning, he placed his hand on his heart. "Kathleen, have

I told you you're gorgeous? I liked the jeans you wore yesterday, but the dress—"

"Aye, you have, and often." She laughed. "And I've thanked you for your kindness each and every time."

"You're very welcome." He stepped closer and tucked a silky tendril behind her ear, his fingers brushing across her high cheekbone. "I applaud your conviction to follow your dreams. You're a determined, sharp-witted businessperson."

She rubbed her palm against the door which had been sanded and stained to a satiny oak finish. "Same as you, aye?"

"Yes, and I don't know if that's a good thing or a bad thing."

"What do you mean?"

"When you're focused on victory at all costs, it's easy to forget the important things in life."

A quiet smile, not quite reaching her eyes, lit her fine-boned face.

He was extremely attracted to her and wondered if it was a good idea to work so closely. He was caught up in her. She was caught up in her business.

He knew the feeling. He'd lived that way most of his adult life. And if he continued analyzing their situation, the fifteen-year difference between them would clutter things up even more.

She extended her hands, apparently unaware of his thoughts. "I hope butter hasn't risen significantly in the Carolinas," she said.

He took her small hands in his. "I'll check in the morning." He perused her flawless figure before his gaze slid to her face. "In the meantime, there's something else we can do besides churn butter."

"What?" She didn't seem to notice the telltale huskiness in his tone.

He pulled her near and pressed a kiss on her hair, her temple, her cheeks.

"Rob …" She gazed up at him and licked her lips. "Maybe we should—"

He swallowed hard. "Kiss?" He framed her face in his hands, stared at her mouth and bent his head.

From the entrance, a crewman's voice called out. The workers were leaving.

Immediately, she stepped back. "I should see them out."

"Why? They can find their way through the front door. They've worked every day since I've been here."

"Aye, but—"

"Kathleen, are you comfortable with us … with me …" Wow, did he ever sound desperate. Quickly, he closed his mouth before he revealed something he'd regret.

"Surely you understand I didn't come to America to find a man."

"And surely you understand there's a magnetism drawing us together."

"Your businesses will be calling you back soon enough, so we shouldn't get too attached to each other."

He tried his most charming grin. "Why not?"

"It's like giving biscuits to a bear."

There went her Irish slang, and he had no notion of what she was talking about. "Meaning?"

"Our being together is a waste of time. Look at what I've undertaken. I can't manage anything more."

He got it. He'd take it slow. She had mountains of tasks, and it was too soon for a commitment.

"Will you take a wee peek at the kitchen in my apartment?" she asked, her tone shifting to businesslike. "The crewmen have enough to complete down here, and one of my shelves needs an adjustment."

"I'm not a carpenter."

"It isn't a complicated job." She led him through the rooms, separated by brick archways, and paused by the staircase. "If you fix the shelf, I'll best the deal with a warm bowl of colcannon."

At his puzzled expression, she clarified, "Mashed potatoes mixed with kale, scallions, milk and butter. And I'll fry you a pan of sausages on the side."

"Free labor for free food," he said. "How can I refuse when I'm ravenous?"

He was ravenous all right. He wanted to hold her, glide his fingers through her strawberry-blond hair, spend hours chatting with her. Kissing her.

As he accompanied her up the creaky wooden stairs, she remarked, "My father never owned anything he couldn't fix."

Rob grimaced. Aware he didn't immediately respond, and likewise aware she was waiting, he contemplated telling her the truth. He'd never been handy with tools, and if she evaluated a man by his hammer wielding abilities, he'd fail miserably.

"That's the way with most men, isn't it?" she added.

Real men fix things. He visualized the slogan—resembling a television commercial.

The tension in his shoulders tightened with each ascending step. He hoped she wouldn't judge him for not being able to hang cabinets or install crown molding, because his reply would be *I can't.* His affluent parents had deemed carpentry beneath them, and encouraged Rob to perform well in school and play sports.

So he had, excelling at both.

And his father had continued to beat him. They'd kept it hidden, presenting a fake façade to their community. Despite the proper upbringing in the proper home, there was no love; only disinterest, indifference, and cruelty. However, they'd filled their home with material possessions, and Rob never lacked the latest tech toy.

After his father had broken Rob's nose once, he'd whipped out his checkbook and bought Rob a Camaro for his sixteenth birthday.

"I can fix this," his father had said, as if a new Camaro could fix a broken nose.

It had come as no surprise his parents didn't approve of his baking career. Although he became a prosperous businessperson, they'd dismissed his achievements.

And now they were gone. A few years earlier, they'd died within months of each other, both from lung cancer. Rob was an only child, and had tried to accept the fact he had failed them, but he never did.

Ten minutes later, he found himself crouched beneath a loose corner shelf in Kathleen's kitchen.

"Can you hand me a hammer, Kathleen?" he asked with a nail held between his teeth.

"Aye," she obliged.

He pinched a second nail between his thumb and index finger, lined the nails up and gave them several sharp whacks. Two nails hammered at once seemed more efficient. Thankfully, she seemed blissfully unaware of his many misses as he attempted to drive the nails into the board and kept slamming his thumb instead. He held in his colorful curses and tried again. Finally, on the fifth attempt, he succeeded.

He stood and wiped wood particles from his jeans. "All set."

There it was. The shelf was secure. Now he could swing a hammer like any of the burly men on Teddy's construction crew.

Her gracious smile filled with appreciation. "What would I do without all this help?"

He prayed she'd narrow her selection down to one helpful person: him. She simply couldn't accomplish this project without *him.*

She slipped off her loafers. "I have something special for us!"

"A wee bit of whiskey?" He peered at her bare feet. "Will we be stomping the whiskey like the Italians stomp grapes for wine?"

"I don't drink," she reminded, skipping to a CD player on the counter. "And what I planned is indeed better."

A lively jig sounded through the kitchen, played by the traditional Celtic instruments of a fiddle, flute, and tin whistle.

She held out her hands, positioning him to face her. "Dance with me, Rob."

He was almost as inept a dancer as he was a carpenter, and he primed the argument on his tongue. "Kathleen, I'm a baker."

"You've repeated that a number of times. And so am I, but I also can dance." She dropped her hands to her sides, and he followed her lead.

"You're Irish," he said. "You've probably danced a jig your entire life."

She wasn't listening. "First, assume the stance." She bounced with the beat, shoulders back and head held high.

He tried to imitate her and carry out her instructions—cross your feet, point your right toe, do a hop, hop back, and lead with your left.

"Leave it to you Irish to make your dance as complicated as drinking tea," he groaned.

She laughed. "Execute the reel straightaway." She whirled him around in a circle, sending her knit dress flying up and exposing shapely bare legs.

He pulled a handkerchief from his pocket to wipe the

sweat from his forehead. He was dizzy, he was breathless. And he was laughing with an abandonment he hadn't felt since he was little.

She giggled, her deep dimples showing. As the jig ended, she collapsed against him. Tears of laughter streamed down her flushed cheeks. "Not so difficult, aye? You danced grand."

"And you're amazing." He caught her tears with his knuckles. In his arms, she was soft and light and he tightened his grip. He was charmed and totally besotted, and he couldn't recall ever being as in love with a woman.

Whoa. Hold that thought.

"I'll teach you the Irish jig whenever you'd like," she was saying. "There're more steps."

"Uh-huh, I'm sure there's a whole book full. I'll put jigs on a back burner for now, but you're an admirable instructor," he said. "And your cooking—"

"Oh, that reminds me." She tore away. "I'll warm the colcannon. That's part of our deal."

"How about a tour first? I spend most of my life in a kitchen."

She tapped a hand to her forehead. "I forgot you haven't seen the rest of my apartment." A slow smile came across her face. "Although saying it's crying for a complete overhaul is an understatement. I've been too busy to entertain decorating ideas, and I admit it's not my strength."

Evidenced by her charming kitchen, she was more than capable. She obviously set high standards for herself.

They wandered through the half-empty rooms—bathroom, hallway, and bedroom. The bare walls were devoid of mementos—no pictures, no window treatments save for shades, no framed photographs of loved ones. The carpet was bland and tattered, the white paint peeling from the ceiling. A chipped farmhouse stool stood as a table beside a worn plaid couch, a knitted blue blanket draped over an end chair. In the corner, wind whistled through cracks in the walls.

Where were her personal belongings? He considered asking, but didn't. She'd admitted to missing Ireland. Possibly she was hesitant to set down permanent roots in America.

Suppose she decided to leave? He captured the troublesome thought and kept it in the forefront of his mind.

"Lovely," he crooned politely as they reentered the kitchen.

"You're too kind." She removed the mashed potato mixture from the refrigerator and transferred it to a pan on the stove.

He grabbed plates and silverware and set the table before coming to stand beside her. "And you work too hard."

"Not any harder than you. Besides—"

"Therefore, I declare tomorrow afternoon a sightseeing holiday."

"Rob, I can't possibly take off an afternoon. Anyway, I'll be knackered."

He quirked an eyebrow.

"Tired. I'll be tired," she said.

"You'll be more productive afterward. What's more, this town is the size of a postage stamp."

"We'll stay in town?"

"For the most part."

She frowned, crunching her delicate eyebrows together. "What's that supposed to mean?"

"It means I plan to show you something first. Then we'll eat dinner at a farm-to-table restaurant that's drawing glowing reviews. Aren't you interested in your local competition?"

"I'm running a teahouse."

"They serve food. You'll be serving food. Maybe new recipe ideas will inspire you."

Ever the entrepreneur, her face lit up. "I guess I can quit at four o'clock."

"Make it three. Where we're going will require a few hours of daylight." He glanced down at her smoky eyes, placed a kiss on her lips, and added a wink.

"Ooh. Sounds mysterious. We're not staying in Roses, then?"

He shrugged. "There's a surprise first."

"I don't usually like surprises. Is this a good surprise?"

"It's a fun surprise," he corrected. "And one I'd like your opinion on."

She gave the colcannon a quick stir, then twisted. "Alright, then. Brilliant."

He smiled. The main thing was that they were going to enjoy an afternoon outside of work. And, by doing so, he'd show her why she should settle in Roses for good.

CHAPTER 9

The following afternoon, Kathleen hummed "Molly Malone", a favorite tune, as Rob pulled up in his candy-red rental car. The afternoon was balmy, foreshadowing the pleasant weather to come.

They'd stopped working at two o'clock after the power had unexpectedly shut off, leaving the crewmen and teahouse in darkness. Fortunately, the electric company had responded and quickly restored power, giving her the opportunity for a hot shower.

She'd taken care with her appearance, dressing in a royal-blue cotton dress with a flared skirt. She paired the dress with brown leather ankle boots and dark tights, topping the outfit with a twill jacket in a light pink print. She'd scrubbed, blow dried, and brushed her long hair until it crackled and shone. Leaving it to lie in loose ringlets around her shoulders, she donned a jaunty straw hat and pinned it in place.

She called out a cheerful greeting as Rob got out of the car. He was at her door before she'd taken a step.

"My beautiful Kathleen." He kissed her warmly on the lips. "Good to see you again."

"You just left my place an hour ago."

He smirked. "And I missed you the entire time." He opened the passenger door for her, and she settled into the plush leather seats.

"Where are we going?" she asked, buckling her seat belt.

He slid into the driver's seat and did the same. "It's a surprise, remember?"

"Rob, I've never liked surprises and—"

"I'll give you two hints." His teasing voice stilled her protests. "It's a town not far from here and it rhymes with toast."

"We're driving to the coast? But we're near the mountains."

Smiling, he pulled to the curb and turned to face her. "I'll give you another hint."

"Alright."

"Boo!"

She jumped, patting her heart. "What on earth? You scared me."

"Sorry." He planted a kiss on her temple, then eased the car back onto the road.

"So now it's presumed I know where we're going?"

He shrugged, an impish expression on his face. "I assumed my clues were useful."

She smiled. "A town rhyming with toast? Boo?" Her smile widened. "Those are clues? Even Sherlock Holmes would have given up."

Their gazes locked—his filled with mischief, hers with a hint of apprehension.

"The surprise is we're driving to Hollan Farms," he said.

"I've never heard of it."

"Teddy and I passed through when we drove from Asheville to Roses." Rob flicked on his blinker and followed a narrow two-lane road, the only traffic a bicycle rider and a lone scooter. "Hollan Farms is a ghost town."

Images of American cowboys and deserted gold rush cities came to mind. "Here? In the Southeast?"

"Technically, a few inhabitants still live there. Sit back and enjoy the ride." He switched on the radio, and James Taylor sang about seeing fire and rain.

They arrived a half hour later, and Rob parked in a graveled car park at the edge of town. Before she could open the door and reach for her straw clutch handbag, he came around and assisted her.

She linked her hand through his arm, their pleasant banter and discerning observations progressing with each step.

"There's a general belief that ghost towns are creepy and haunted," he said. "From my research, this town is none of these."

"Except it does looks abandoned." She pointed to a string of empty storefronts. "It doesn't take a genius to realize no one has lived here for a while."

"Yes, there's that."

Her cheeks warmed as he regarded her, his gaze moving to her lips before he took her in his arms and kissed her.

She was with him far too often. He was the picture of who and what she'd intended to avoid—a good-looking man sharing precious, remarkable moments with her.

Risky, risky, risky. If she continued along this path, eventually her heart would be broken.

But this was Rob, and he was different.

Aye. Different all right. He was too appealing, too perceptive, too much of a distraction.

Too much of an *attraction.*

A light breeze caused her straw hat to flap, and she placed one hand on top of her head to steady it. Trees on every street corner blossomed, sending tiny white petals floating through the air.

As they wound through a forsaken alleyway, Rob seemed to take in every element of the buildings—the worn scalloped awning on the supermarket, abandoned café tables outside a bistro, an ornamental stone fountain. She imagined water bursting from the basin, children playing around it, street vendors selling bunches of flowers and delectable coffee and desserts.

"This was a boomtown, a resort boasting a healing hot spring, luxurious spa, and top-rate restaurants," Rob said. "The town went belly up because of the economic downturn a few years ago. Sadly, the anticipated clientele—middle America—could no longer afford spa vacations."

She slowed to peer through a dusty café window. Chairs and tables were arranged in the middle of the floor, menus stacked by the receptionist's booth as if frozen in time.

"And the hot spring?" she inquired.

"What about it?"

"Where is it?"

"It still runs through the center of town."

The sky changed to a dove gray, and the sun disappeared. A minute later, a heavy rain shower caught her sleeves with drops of water.

"Hold on to your hat," Rob joked. He grabbed her hand and led her on a race through the streets.

"This happens in Ireland constantly," she said, winded and laughing. "One minute it's sunny, the next, rain is bucketing down."

They ducked beneath the canopied entrance of a once impressive hotel, the windows reflecting a marbled tile entryway and carpet at least ten years old.

"It storms and rains on many hot afternoons in Miami too," Rob said.

Water dripped from the brim of her hat, a puddle forming at their feet. "Except Ireland's weather is a wee bit cooler than Miami, to be sure."

"You think?"

"I know for certain." Her hand was still clasped in his warm one. This close, with his warm blue eyes framed by thick brows and his ever-present smile, he exuded self-assurance. Not arrogant the way some men she'd dated carried themselves, more interested in their lives than anything she had to say.

As she gazed up at Rob, she noticed his nose had been broken at least once. Tenderly, she ran her finger across the bridge. "What happened?" she asked softly.

"He liked whiskey and bourbon and cigarettes."

"Who?"

"My father." Rob was silent for several beats. "The combination was frightening when he was angry."

"Your father." She mulled the two words in her mind. Rob rarely spoke about his family or his past. "Did he ... break your nose?"

"Yes."

"So, he beat you?"

"Often."

"Oh, Rob." What could she say? She knew from Clara's brother, Seamus, how alcohol twisted a person's life into a roller-coaster, the ups and downs catching loved ones in a virtual whirlwind of emotions. Inevitably, wreckage and despair followed.

"It happened years ago. Decades, literally." Rob spoke so softly she wasn't sure she heard him. She thought he dabbed at his eyes.

She pictured him as a small boy, chubby, sweet-faced, an infectious beam in his deep-set eyes. "It's alright," she finally said.

"What I remember most is the smell of my father's whiskey and cigarette breath, and the sight of him asleep at the oak desk in his study, an empty liquor bottle lying beside him. I tried to please him, I really did."

The neediness in Rob's voice warmed a secret place in her heart. Perhaps that was why he'd tried so hard all these years to succeed—in his effort to satisfy parents who didn't care. He was a pleaser, thinking of everyone except himself.

"I'm sorry." Something inside prompted her to squeeze his hand and offer reassurance. "The future is what matters."

They stood quiet, the steady rain beating down on the hotel's canopy. He stared at her so long a shiver coursed through her. He trusted her enough to share his heart-breaking memories.

Truly, he cared about her.

And she, in turn, cared about him. Trusted him.

More than cared. More than trusted. She was falling in love with him.

No. Not here. Not now.

Then where, exactly? And when? All she needed to do was gaze at him. The confirmation stood directly in front of her—with his every intention, and devotion shining from his brilliant blue eyes. Somehow, in the madness of two different worlds, they'd found each other.

Knowing her rain-dampened cheeks were a hot pink, she broke the spell and spun to peer through the hotel's grimy window. She tented her hands and read the scrawled sign posted in the lobby. "We are open to patrons during the summer months."

"Wow," Rob said. "Business is booming."

She laughed and pivoted. "For who, exactly?"

"I don't know. It might be an old sign."

"Didn't you say a handful of people still live in Hollan Farms?"

"Yes, but they wouldn't stay at the hotel."

"So, where are they?"

He shrugged. Gently, he wiped rain droplets off her chin. "They're probably in Asheville for the day."

"The entire population?"

"The entire population of ten."

The rain stopped as suddenly as it had started. He kept hold of her hand as they continued their exploration, answering her speculative questions with speculative answers. Eventually, they crossed a rickety wooden bridge.

The famed babbling hot spring nestled beside budding trees and shrubs, and Kathleen caught her breath at the exquisite sight. With mountain views in the distance, the scene could have been a page removed from a travel brochure advertising tranquility.

"Beautiful," she murmured. "Like a fairy-tale reproduction of what real life should be."

"Zen."

At her raised eyebrows, he explained, "Zen is Japanese slang for serenity."

She gazed upward and sighed. White, wispy clouds floated above, drifting leisurely. No rush for the clouds. Nature was never in a hurry. If only she could harness that same inner peace.

Directly opposite the sun, a muted band of colors formed an arc. "Look, Rob." She pointed. "A rainbow!"

"I'll snap a photo."

"Quick, before it disappears."

He pulled his cell-phone from his pocket, stepped beside her, and snapped a selfie of them framed by the rainbow.

She was too enchanted by this fascinating town to object.

"You're prettier than any rainbow." Rob hung his arm around her shoulders. "But I can delete the photo if—"

"No, of course not." She wanted to relish the growing

attraction between them, to spend every precious minute with him. Everything about him was appealing—each shared glance, the feel of his callused hand around hers, his agreeable, mellow nature.

She peered at the sky. Already, the rainbow was fading. A homesickness she hadn't felt in a while enveloped her.

"Are you okay?" he asked.

"I'm fine." She brushed her fingers across her eyes. "Oftentimes, the rainbows in Ireland are brilliant."

"Rainbows are brilliant in America too, Kathleen. And Roses is your new home."

Here. With me.

The words dangled between them.

"Do you desire a soak, my lady?" he asked when they reached the edge of the hot spring. "You know, all those healing powers …"

"I didn't bring my swimsuit," she joked.

"A pity." He moved behind her and wrapped his hands around her waist, nuzzling her neck. She turned, considering, then stood on her tiptoes and kissed him.

He drew an inward breath and folded her in his arms. She wrapped her hands around his nape.

This was decisive.

She was done worrying about dating, or relationships, or whether this was the right time. Because here was Rob, a man she trusted. She loved the way his lips were firm, yet tender and enticing. He was so good to her, polite, calm, respectful.

When the kiss ended, he whispered, "You have no idea how often I think about you."

Likewise. He was in her thoughts every minute.

He beckoned her to dip her hands into the water with him.

"I read that famous actors and actresses who visited here often immersed themselves in the healing waters," he said.

Kathleen splashed water on her face. "Whether the spring is healing or not, this town is delightful."

"I agree." He looked around, pensive, deliberating. "And it's for sale."

"What is?" She aimed her gaze across the street. "The hotel?"

"The town."

Playfully, she swatted him. "A town can't be for sale."

"Sure it can."

The whole town was for sale.

And Rob had a gleam in his eyes she instantly recognized. Once an entrepreneur, always an entrepreneur.

"How much?" she asked.

"I've done some investigating. Plus, Candee's a real estate agent, which is helpful."

"How much?" she repeated.

"Several million dollars."

He might as well have stated several trillion dollars; the amount was so removed from her stratosphere.

"Rob, surely you're not thinking of buying a ... town."

He chuckled. "Teddy and Candee voiced the same reservation."

"What about your bakeries?"

"I'm putting them up for sale. I'm retiring."

She touched a hand to her parted lips. "You'd sell Rob's Marvelous Muffins?"

"I'll keep the name and unload the buildings, retail spaces and my condo. I'll start the paperwork when I fly to Miami."

"Is this wise? You've established a wonderful reputation. What about your recipes, your customer base—"

His jaw set. "All too much work."

"Compared to renovating a town?" She couldn't find a

coherent sentence to sputter. "Along with the actual price, it'll take several more millions to fix all the buildings."

"True." Lazily, he stroked a stray ringlet falling across her shoulder.

She stepped back. "Isn't that a lot of money?"

"Yes. However, Hollan Farms has one thing Miami lacks."

His words caught, and she looked up at him. The entire afternoon had followed its own course. And in his explanation, she recognized a deep emotion. Commitment.

"Healing spring water?" she half teased.

"Guess again."

"Rob, I …" She'd forgotten her guesses, anyway. When she was with him, she forgot all her troubles.

She knew he watched her, so she ventured, "The town offers dilapidated cafés just waiting for your marvelous muffins?"

"Nope."

"What could Hollan Farms possibly offer that isn't in Miami?"

"You." He brought her into his arms, bent his head, and thoroughly kissed her. "I'm planning to move to Roses permanently."

WHEN THEIR TOUR of the town ended, the sun hung low in the sky, the beginnings of a sunset casting vivid purple and orange hues that shadowed the derelict buildings. By the time they arrived at the farm-to-table restaurant, stars blanketed a clear night sky.

Rob's admission that he would sell all he'd built in order to be close to her had successfully breached the last of her defenses. Here she'd assumed the wall barricading her heart had been honed to perfection and nothing could penetrate it.

And it had been so, until she'd met this honest, mature gentleman. Until the impossible had occurred.

She'd fallen for him, and there was no turning back.

"Are you hungry?" he inquired.

"I'm starving, actually."

"Next time we go to the hot spring, we'll pack a picnic."

Next time. A promise of shared experiences to come. Celebrations.

Seeing the restaurant's parking lot packed with cars, she remarked, "We may not be eating here tonight."

"I made reservations," he said.

His cell-phone pinged. He darted a glance at the caller ID and scowled. "Sorry, Kathleen, I need to take this. One of my managers—"

She drew in a breath before a sharp retort rolled from her tongue. *Rob,* she wanted to say. *Must your business always come first?*

After a clipped exchange, Rob ended the call.

Scents of smoked bacon and fresh-baked rolls wafted from the doorway as they ascended the restaurant's stairs. Inside, the walls were decorated in cherry-wood paneling. Candlelight and a pianist playing soft background music— well-known Broadway show tunes—completed the understated elegance.

As Rob hung her jacket, Kathleen removed her floppy hat and peered at her outfit, grateful she'd worn a dress.

When they were seated, a black-clad waiter brought menus, explaining the food was fresh and locally sourced, while he poured glasses of sparkling water.

She enjoyed an exquisite meal of a seared chicken breast served on a bed of roasted mushrooms and cherry tomatoes, while Rob opted for the grilled beef tenderloin with spinach and spaghetti squash.

For dessert, she ordered black coffee and a cherry fruit

cobbler. She forked a piece of the crust and chewed discerningly.

"How is it?" Rob asked. He'd ordered bread pudding filled with frozen grapes, and raisin rum ice cream on the side.

She placed the fork near her plate and patted her lips with the linen napkin. "Surprisingly mediocre. Yours?"

"The same." He toyed with the pudding, then scooped up a spoonful of ice cream. "Odd, because dinner was delicious. I wonder if they outsource their desserts because I know a certain woman who bakes a heavenly brown bread." A not-so-secret smile appeared on his lips.

Chuckling, she shook her head. "I have enough on my plate baking bread and scones for my patrons-to-be. What about you?"

"I'm retiring, remember?"

Sure, by buying and restoring a ghost town boasting a hot spring, grocery store, hotel, and who knew what else.

As she sipped her coffee, she felt an unexplainable surge of pride for his tenaciousness. Although he'd told her he didn't have a bit of Irish blood in him—his surname, Taylor, being French and Scottish—he was as sharp-witted as any Irishman.

"What's the finest dessert you've ever tasted?" she asked.

In the softness of candlelight, his face appeared younger. He looked rested and happy. "Your brown bread."

She smiled over the rim of her cup. "No, really."

"There's a mom-and-pop restaurant near Asheville. I dined there with Teddy a while back, and the owners specialize in homemade apple cobblers topped with a flaky crust. I'll take you there some time." He leaned in. "What about you?"

"Ah, well, in Ireland, any coffee shop or café will likely serve desserts prepared in-house."

"I'd like to visit Ireland someday," he said quietly.

Don't go there, she thought. A small part of her demanded she stay on track—launching an up-and-coming teahouse in America. That meant no distractions.

But then, she'd already made her decision. With Rob, her world had changed. They could enjoy America and Ireland together, as a team, as a couple, as two people devoted to each other.

She sat back in the tufted chair, moving in time to the pianist's rendition of the upbeat "I Could Have Danced All Night" from *My Fair Lady*.

She tilted back her head, her smile lighthearted. "It would be an honor to show you my country, Rob."

"I can't wait."

She inhaled, treasuring the moment. She'd made the correct choice coming to Roses, and she wanted Rob in her life.

The way he smiled back at her told her everything. It warmed her weary heart, and there was no mistaking the love in his expression.

CHAPTER 10

"I'll depart for Miami tomorrow," Rob told Kathleen a few days after they'd dined at the farm-to-table restaurant. They stood on the front porch of her teahouse on a brisk day in early March. A sharp breeze ruffled the burgundy striped awning that had recently been installed.

She swallowed and avoided his gaze. "Seven days seems like forever."

"I'm merely a few hours away by plane. In the meantime, I have a gift so you won't forget me." He withdrew a silver-foil-wrapped box from his sport jacket and handed it to her.

Solemnly, he watched her open a black velvet box and snap open the lid. Inside was a Victorian heart-shaped skeleton key locket on a cable chain, plated in twenty-four carat gold.

"Thank you," she said. "It's beautiful."

"For a beautiful woman." He secured the chain around her neck. "My Irish queen, you hold the key to my heart. Always remember that."

She laughed. "Fit for a queen, aye?"

"Yes." He nodded. "Open the locket."

She popped the magnetic closure, and all laughter vanished from her face. She studied the miniature photo tucked inside—the one he'd taken of them at Hollan Farms with the stunning rainbow in the background.

"Turn the locket over," he instructed.

On the back was inscribed: 1-800-IRELAND.

Tears welled in her eyes. "Thank you," she said again.

"I hope you will always think of me when you wear it."

"Every day."

"That's what I like to hear." He embraced her in a loving hold. Against her cheek, his chest was warm and comforting, his heartbeat steady and sure. "I'll return well before your grand opening. I promise, and I never go back on my word."

He was considerate and compassionate, intuitive to her feelings.

She acknowledged his promise, although tears burned. "I'll miss you," she said.

"Not as much as I'll miss you."

She declined his pocket handkerchief that he offered, her thoughts scattering.

When he was near, she felt treasured. Now these crucial hours leading up to March 17 would continue without him.

Well, she'd steel her shoulders and deal with it. He had a business to run. So did she. Furthermore, she was a resourceful entrepreneur. Rob had told her so himself.

He pressed a kiss on her lips. "I'll call as soon as I land in Miami." His gaze flicked to the crewmen busily making adjustments to the wood floor in one of the dining rooms. "Teddy, Candee, Keiran, and Desiree are all around, so you won't be alone."

Despite his assurances, a moment of sadness went through her, just long enough to cause her chest to ache. She was truly alone now.

Woodenly, she nodded. "Aye."

And with that, the next day he was gone.

As the week passed, she enlisted Teddy's crew as taste testers while she perfected scones and breads. Happily, they obliged.

Candee designed a high-quality menu, and aprons were ordered to match Kathleen's teahouse logo. At the last minute, the crewmen erected a pergola to the outside seating area, where bottled water, tea, and fruit juices would be sold.

Kathleen stationed a NOW HIRING sign near the entrance of the teahouse, and several applicants immediately responded. Interviewing the bright-faced candidates left her invigorated and hopeful.

However, various decisions still loomed. Would customers prefer high tea or a more casual atmosphere? Parsnips in their soup or a traditional creamy broccoli? Spot-on decisions meant enthusiastic regulars, and she counted on Rob's daily answers to her texts.

As the days flew forward, two catastrophes occurred.

First, the large dough mixer wasn't expected to arrive on time after all.

Forcing herself to sound calm and unemotional, she phoned Rob.

"You have countertop hand mixers, right?" he asked.

"Aye, and a dough proofer and all the bakeware."

"Tell the two assistants you hired to use what's available. They're qualified, correct?"

"Which brings me to my second catastrophe." She could hardly voice the words. "One quit before she started because she said the start-up wage is too low. The other is in university and her work days are limited."

"Keep looking."

"I am. There may be a third applicant. Her name is Nancy, and she's enthusiastic and eager."

"How old is she?"

"Twenty-something. She's willing to work alongside me, doesn't mind long hours, and told me that my teahouse is unique and special."

"She's a keeper. People like that are hard to find, so train her well and take any spare minute to invest in her development. And don't forget to phone Keiran too. He's a block away."

"I did. O'Malley's is busier than ever and he can't spare anyone this close to St. Patrick's Day. Teddy has even bussed a few tables there to help Keiran out."

Rob blew out a sigh. "Unfortunately, being short-staffed is typical in this industry."

"Short-staffed is one thing. No staffed is another."

"Part-time employees aren't dependable. I'd refer a couple of mine, but with my stores for sale, everyone is in an upheaval. Many of my steady workers are seeking employment elsewhere."

"Didn't you assure them that their jobs were secure?"

"I tried, although new owners may bring aboard different people."

She paused. "Rob, can I ask you another question?"

"Certainly."

"Should I urge my customers to place their cell-phones in containers when they walk in? You know, to strengthen community, and encourage family conversations."

Through the phone, she heard a man speaking to Rob.

"Sorry Kathleen, it's David," Rob said.

"The cow guy?"

"Yes, and it's apparently urgent. Hang on." Rob muffled the phone. He addressed David's question, then came back on the line. "This place is like a zoo today. What were you saying?"

"Nothing." Kathleen's grip on her phone tightened. "I'll sort it out myself."

"Sorry," he said softly. "Once this place is sold, we'll be together."

When? Selling a huge commercial operation wouldn't be a matter of a few days. It would take weeks, maybe months. Maybe years.

She'd always found herself cheered after talking with Rob. However, her chin quivered as she felt her safeguards being swept aside. She relied on him, but he had enough on his hands without her constant barrage of questions. In the interim, she needed to trust her own business sense.

She inhaled deeply. "Do you remember Sean, my coworker at The Ground Café?"

"The guy who is supposedly interested in quitting his manager job in Ireland to lend you a hand in America?"

"I wouldn't put it that way, Rob," she corrected. "He isn't *supposedly* interested. He is interested and assured he won't accept a salary from me. Plus, he'd work full-time, so there's no dependability issue."

"You've discussed your last-minute problems with him, plus he'll work for free?" She could almost see Rob's eyes narrowing. "Why?"

"Because he's a friend." She bristled. "He's been nothing but supportive. He rang me again last night."

"And now he's phoning you as well as texting?"

"Only twice since you left. He's as experienced as you are."

"Your brogue is thickening, and you sound defensive, which is never a good sign." There was an inexplicable seriousness in Rob's tone, coupled with frustration. "And what did you tell Mr. Sean?"

"I told him I was handling things well on my own,

although these days I'm thinking I can use his support. He's ringing me tomorrow morning."

"Sounds like you talk with this guy more than you talk with me."

"Don't be ridiculous. You and I chat every day. It's just that you're … preoccupied." She couldn't remember the last time her conversation with Rob hadn't been interrupted at least once. And Sean was 100 percent available—and always sympathizing with her.

"Kathleen." Rob allowed the silence between them to go on for twice as long as she expected. "There's a lot involved here in Miami."

"I know." She squeezed her eyes shut. "And I should be more understanding."

He didn't say yes or no. Instead, he continued, "Several of my managers expressed interest in purchasing the entire business. That's heartening, because they've been with me for years and I trust them to maintain the quality. However, bank loan applications are time-consuming. Not to mention, my bakeries are all still running."

She needed him. Now. Didn't he realize that?

She shook her head. She was being selfish.

"I understand," she said quietly, although she heard the edge in her tone.

"Remember our ghost town. Our life together. Remember us."

Us.

The dovelike caress threading his words caused a delicious shiver up her spine.

"I'll remember." She gave a weary smile into the phone.

Hollan Farms. An empty shell of a town. Despite Rob's assurances, she felt similar to that town. Abandoned.

When her cell-phone rang at dawn, she recognized Sean's

number on the caller ID. And when he asked if she required back-up relief, she answered with one word.

Aye.

He was capable. He was more than eager. And they'd worked closely before.

ON A RAIN-SOAKED afternoon a couple days afterward, Sean appeared in Roses. His flights from Dublin to Asheville were brilliant, he assured. He'd hired an Uber for the final leg to Roses.

"You quit your job at The Ground Café?" Kathleen inquired as he met her under the front awning. Despite the heavy travel he looked well-rested, his olive-camouflage jacket and black pants washed and pressed.

"Aye. Howya." He placed his luggage on the stoop and grasped her in a fierce hug. "I'm tired of working for someone else."

"You'll work for me now."

He didn't answer. A shadow crossed his hard-lined face.

"Well, travel certainly agrees with you." She pondered her statement as she regarded him. "When I flew the transatlantic flight, it took me several days to recover from jet lag."

"Kathleen, I must confess." His gaze darted. "I landed in Boston last week."

"Boston?" With keen effort, she controlled her temper while drawing a slow breath. "I assumed you were in Ireland when you rang me."

"I figured I was off to America, anyway. A few days earlier didn't matter."

"And if I didn't accept your bid to help me?"

"Don't know." He waved his hands airily. His hazel eyes darkened. "I may have stayed in Boston, although I knew you'd come round eventually if I kept badgering."

Typical Sean. He'd always hassled big-hearted Danny Brady at The Ground Café, requesting weekends off or extended paid holidays until Danny agreed.

"You're obviously a pro at badgering," she said.

"I suppose I am."

She couldn't keep from staring at him. His medium-length dark hair had been styled into a kinky perm.

"Any comments?" He finger combed the curls. "A man perm is all the rage."

"It's ..." She stopped herself before saying *hysterically funny*, assuming he wouldn't appreciate the humor.

"Foxy?" he questioned.

"Aye, especially combined with your dark beard."

"*Go raibh míle maith agat.*"

Thanks a million. The familiar Irish words brought a rush of tears to her eyes.

"Can you recommend a place in town where I can rent a room?" he asked.

"There's a splendid bed-and-breakfast not far from here."

"And a pub with good craic?" He stepped too close, completely disregarding her personal space. "I'm definitely fond of parties."

She moved backward, remembering the times he'd reported to The Ground Cafe after going out on the lash and drinking. Although she'd often smelled alcohol on his breath, it hadn't seemed to affect his performance.

"If you're in search of lively banter," she pointed down the street, "Keiran O'Malley's pub is walking distance from here. Just don't drink on the days you're working."

"Wouldn't think of it."

"Do you remember Keiran's cousin William?" she asked.

"I do." His gaze leveled on her. "He won your affection and took you away from me."

"We're all just friends, Sean."

"I'd like us to be more than friends, Kathleen. Surely you must know that."

"Sean. No. Although I'm thankful for your support."

"Gotcha. Loud and clear." He raised his hands in feigned surrender. "As soon as I'm a wee bit settled, I'll visit Keiran's pub on my off days." His small hazel eyes left hers to regard the teahouse's green painted shingles. "Your place looks brilliant. The color reminds me of Ireland."

"Do you think so? Decorating isn't my forte, I just wanted an old European touch. Fortunately, my friend Candee guided me. I couldn't even choose curtains until she carried over several fabric swatches and I finally decided on a jewel-tone floral."

"Candee is your real estate agent?"

"Aye. Her husband, Teddy, is my contractor." Kathleen blew out a breath. "I'm trying hard to resist the impulse to text her every time there's a decorating problem."

"Luckily, here I am to solve everything." He picked up his luggage, and they stepped inside, the front bell tinkling to announce their arrival.

"Thanks for coming. You're an asset, Sean."

"It's because our Irish work ethic is first rate."

She grinned, turning her attention to the shelves teeming with tea. "Today I'm trying to decide how many loose-leaf blends to serve my customers."

"Less is better to keep the quality up."

"Sean, there are over 250 teas to choose from."

"From the looks of it, you've bought them all." He planted his hands on his bony hips. "Stick with a basic selection of twelve."

"I planned a high tea every day at four o'clock. Is that too much?"

"Roses is a little-bitty town," he said. "Compromise and

serve high tea on weekends only. You'll end up failing if you overextend yourself."

"You're right," she said.

His boots clicked across the wood floors, and she glided her hand over a lavish tea service she'd polished until the silver gleamed. "I can't believe you flew such a long way for me."

"My pleasure." Lightly, he brushed a curl coming loose from her pony tail in much the same way when they'd worked double shifts together and were exhausted at the end of the day. "You remember I'm the adventurous sort. Like you."

She also remembered he used to point that out a lot. *Spirited go-getters intent on success,* he'd say. Somehow, the words didn't sound as flattering as they once did.

IN THE ENSUING DAYS, Sean inched his way into becoming an integral part of every decision, from improving providers' terms to mounting a decorative box next to each table for cell-phones.

He was shrewd, often voicing her objectives before she did, or latching on to an idea and expanding it. He repeatedly pointed out that her concepts were comparable to The Ground Café's. Therefore, when she described a problem with the teas or scones, he immediately chimed in with eleventh-hour solutions.

Rob phoned numerous times, and she played phone tag with him. She yearned for his quick grin, the sound of his deep voice, his warm-hearted reassurances. However, immersed in a whirlwind of activity, the hours passed all too quickly.

Another snag, Rob texted the evening after Sean's arrival.

I'm coming, but delayed a few more days. I should be in Roses by Friday.

Understandable, she replied, noting Friday was a week away. *I'll send photos of my new menu.*

Sean watched while she texted Rob and smiled knowingly.

"I'm here for you," was all he said.

The following day, Kathleen went through every nook in her teahouse for elements she might have missed. Lightly, she traced her fingers over the herbal tea baskets, honey dispensers, and a row of clear glass pitchers. Teddy's crew had completed the renovation, and the place was quiet, save for a collection of Irish tunes playing on the CD.

Everything in the teahouse was unique and stylish, a far cry from the greasy, cramped, and gloomy interior she'd first encountered. She knew Rob would be impressed.

Rob.

She'd meant to send him photos of the menu. In the flurry of activity, she'd forgotten, falling into bed at night too weary to think. She'd do it in the morning.

"What will the children drink?" Sean came up behind her and interrupted her thoughts.

"What children?"

"Your customers will bring in their wee ones. You'll want to keep them content and occupied."

"I can serve hot cocoa."

"What about a fun tea experience?" He inclined his head. "Brew decaffeinated tea and give it an unusual name—like cinnamon toast tea served in a cup named Chip."

"A chipped cup?"

"From *Beauty and the Beast*," he prompted.

"Oh, right." She smiled. "Brilliant. Let's include that name on the chalkboard."

. . .

LATER THE SAME DAY, a $6000 invoice arrived for the double-deck gas convection oven. It was stamped OVERDUE.

Kathleen scanned the bill and gasped.

Sean peered over her shoulder. "Troubles?"

"How can the supplier expect payment if I'm not even open yet?" She set the invoice on the counter and began mixing dough for wheat bread. For her, baking was therapeutic and gave her something to do with her hands. "Financially, I'm stretched to the max."

"You can't apply for another loan?"

"I'm considered an upstart, and banks don't risk their money. I put up my parent's home in County Galway that was deeded to me upon their death as collateral. After $200,000 dollars, I'm tapped out."

He lifted a dark eyebrow, then perused the letter accompanying the invoice. "The company can shut you down if you can't remit."

"Naturally I pay my bills. Just not until the teahouse opens."

"I can help."

She placed the dough into the electric mixer and switched it on. "Sean, I refuse to accept your money. I know you're not a rich man."

The electricity blew out with a snap. The lights switched off, and the mixer stopped.

"Again?" she groaned. "Teddy said we may have an electrical issue if this keeps up, although the power company blames the problem on the new lines being dug in the area. I hope they're right, because I don't have an extra five thousand—"

"At present, it's an easy fix," Sean assured, finding the breaker box and switching the power back on. Once the mixer started running again, he showed up beside her.

"Kathleen, I have a business proposition for you," he said.

"I already had one."

"From your hotshot Miami boyfriend?"

She winced. She'd confided to Sean about Rob's job proposal. She wished she hadn't. A day hadn't gone by when Sean didn't bring up Rob, and his remarks were never flattering.

"I'm not selling my teahouse and setting back to Ireland with my tail between my legs," she declared, "so don't tell me to give up."

"We Irish have more pride than that."

There it was again. *We versus them.* The Irish versus the Americans, the bankers, even Teddy's crewmen if Sean disagreed with their work. He constantly implied the Irish were underdogs and appealed to her sense of patriotism.

She shut off the mixer, wrested the dough from the bowl, and began kneading. "What are you saying?"

"We share a passion for this type of place." He sidled closer. Instinctively, she moved back a step. "You and I worked under brass-hat Brady and watched him make difficult decisions."

"So?"

"So let's face the truth. You can't run a business. You're too emotionally involved." His tone challenged with a hint of mockery. "And there are numerous details, far too many for one person. You're in over your head, luv. Hey, you can't even make a decision about curtains without help."

Luv. She let the word go by.

She kept her head down while she rolled out the dough, then dusted her flour-stained hands along the edges of her apron. "As you obviously guessed, my specialty isn't interior design."

"This isn't about decorating. This is about realizing your strengths and admitting your weaknesses."

Rather than argue, she agreed, because she knew arguing

with him was useless. He was always willing to fight, and she didn't have the energy. Despite the never-ending work hours, her problems continued to mushroom. Somewhere along the way, she'd begun to feel powerless.

Maybe Sean was right. Her corporate sense wasn't strong. Sure, she'd been in positions of management, but that was different from owning a company where every choice meant financial loss and subsequent failure.

She sank onto a high-backed chair. "What are you suggesting?"

"As I said, I'm offering a firm proposition and subsequent solution."

Her eyebrows flicked upward, measuring him. "Which is?"

"I'll buy into your business." He watched her closely as he pulled up a chair. "Your financial worries will end, and you'll be free to bake and serve customers—the services you did best at The Ground Café."

"Your terms ..."

He slid his chair closer, then stretched out his legs. "A 60/40 split. In my favor."

"Absolutely not." Firmly, she shook her head. "I did all the groundwork."

"I'll continue your vision going forward, so don't go flashing those blustery eyes at me." With both hands on his knees, he leaned forward. "I'll take over all business aspects, financial and otherwise, and you can concentrate on a successful opening day."

"Sean, this is a difficult conversation." She rubbed the middle of her forehead and closed her eyes. "Give me time to consider."

"Rest assured I have your best interests at heart. In fact, I'll draw up the necessary papers." He lifted her chin. "It's best for everyone, aye?"

A heaviness invaded her body. Quieting, she gazed down at her rumpled apron, her washed-out jeans, and tried not to twist her hands. She was cornered, and her teahouse deserved no less than the best. She surveyed her supply of china cups and saucers stacked neatly on the shelves, the double-deck gas convection oven. What would happen if she lost her oven because of nonpayment? Her teahouse couldn't survive without the main oven and a large dough mixer, and she'd run out of funds.

"I'll think about it," she replied.

But what about Nancy, the new girl she'd hired, who seemed genuinely interested in learning the tea business?

Kathleen's mind whirled in a thousand different directions.

FOUR MORE DAYS WENT BY. Four more nights she spent staring at the ceiling in her shabby apartment, seeking the serenity of sleep before it vanished, forcing prolonged hours of insomnia and torturous deliberations.

And somewhere along the way, she stopped communicating with Rob altogether.

CHAPTER 11

On Wednesday of the following week, Rob strode over the tiny white blossoms lacing the front porch of Kathleen's teahouse. He knocked, then opened the wooden door. A tiny bell announced his arrival, though no one acknowledged him.

He'd texted his flight information to Kathleen the night before and she hadn't replied. In fact, he hadn't heard a word from her in several days. A quick query to Candee assured Kathleen was well, albeit "busy beyond words". Still, the silence had prompted him to return to Roses a couple days early.

Despite his focus on Miami and the mountain of paperwork yet to be signed, he congratulated himself. He'd successfully sold his business to a group of managers who'd worked in his bakeries for years. They'd pooled their funds, the bank loans were secured, and the closing was slated in a month.

"Sorry, fella. We're not open until St. Patrick's Day." A pencil-thin man sporting a dark beard and curly hair sat at a round table in the center of the main dining room. He was unmistakably Irish, his dialect quick, his sentences running together. He straightened from his sprawling position and refilled his glass of iced tea. "Come back Saturday for our grand opening."

"I'm aware of when March seventeenth is." Disregarding the man's hostile gaze, Rob strode further into the room.

"You Americans are smarter than people give you credit for."

"Who are you?" Rob demanded.

"Sean."

"Yeah, I figured."

"You?" came Sean's clipped inquiry.

"Rob."

"Aye. Without a doubt." Sean's derisive grin followed his flippant acknowledgement. He lifted his glass. "My only defense against the warm weather. In Ireland, March is a cold, rainy month. Here, the sun shines almost continuously and it's a bit warm for me."

"You'd melt in Miami then," Rob said. "How long have you been in Roses?"

"A few days."

Rob corralled his anger, focusing on the welcoming environment of the teahouse. The stunning renovation was a treasure trove. Orderly shelves displayed simple fruit jellies and preserves, and the counter was stocked with freshly ground coffee and an assortment of loose herbal teas in glass jars. The entire space was airy and bright. On the corner of each table, he noted a container.

Sean followed his gaze. "We added those for cell-phones. Kathleen believes in conversation with no interruptions."

Rob grimaced, recalling the number of times his chats with Kathleen had been cut off by his familiar cell-phone ping.

"Hungry?" Sean raised a silver tray laden with croissants.

"Nope." Rob avoided meeting the man's assessing stare. "Where is she?"

Sunshine eased through the floral curtains, lighting the cozy atmosphere, offset by candles shimmering along an antique sideboard. The cashmere comfort of a welcoming warmth enveloped him. In that instant, Rob saw the realization of Kathleen's remarkable achievement.

Well done, Kathleen.

"She's baking another Keiran O'Malley recipe in her apartment, because she prefers her small oven," Sean was saying. "Keiran has Irish relatives, you see."

"I'm aware."

"He's a decent bloke and has made me feel right at home. His pub is fierce and just the thing after a knackered day in a scorching kitchen."

"And I'm interested in Kathleen, not you." Rob crossed his arms. "I'll wait for her here and you can be on your way."

Since he'd entered, Rob had been struggling with an escalating annoyance, standing by while Sean lazily drank iced tea and tamped up croissant crumbs from his plate with his fingers. He felt like a panhandler waiting to be granted an audience with a queen.

"I'd suggest *you* should be the one on your way." Sean's sharp voice cut through Rob's thoughts. "You're acting like a Holy Joe coming to her rescue, but as you can see, we're ready for our opening and things have gone swimmingly. And we did it all without brainy old you."

"Excuse me?" In three strides, Rob closed the distance between them. "*We're* ready? *Our* opening? What's going on here?"

"I'll blame your questions on poor hearing because of your age and not poor listening. As you Americans speak frankly, I'll frame this so that you understand. Crack on and leave."

"Don't tell me what to do," Rob warned. "This isn't your place." He yanked out his cell-phone and typed Kathleen a text. *Where are you? I'm standing in your dining room.*

"On the contrary, it *is* my place." Sean examined his well-manicured fingernails. "Kathleen has agreed to make me her business partner. I'm here for the long haul."

For a moment, Rob couldn't trust himself to reply, his brain registering disbelief. His narrowed gaze examined Sean's blasé expression.

"I don't believe it. Kathleen is self-reliant."

Sean shrugged. "She's going in a different direction."

"Indeed?" Rob inquired. "Tell me more."

He'd been gone only a short while and Sean had triumphantly wormed his way back into her life. Slowly, something inside Rob began to crumble. While he was working out details and selling everything for her, she was handing over her business to this pompous Irishman.

He recalled his phone call with Kathleen when she'd sprung to Sean's defense.

"Do you remember Sean, my coworker at The Ground Café?" she'd asked.

"The guy who is supposedly interested in quitting his manager job in Ireland to lend you a hand in America?"

"I wouldn't put it that way, Rob. Sean isn't supposedly interested. He is interested and assured he won't accept a salary if he were to come here."

Rob scrubbed a hand over his face. He should've known Sean wouldn't waste a second quitting his job, flying over the Atlantic Ocean and coming to Kathleen's rescue. Nevertheless, she considered Sean a friend, so Rob was willing to endure the rest of the exchange for her sake.

"What are the terms of this offer?" Rob asked. "Because I can make her a better one."

"Can you? Mine is a 60/40 split."

"She'd agree to that?" Rob barked a laugh. "I'm surprised."

"We've always been brilliant together, and I'm her new fella. She's a fine thing, isn't she?"

Rob grappled with a stab of jealousy. "I can afford to give her the world," he said quietly.

"Your wealth doesn't impress me or Kathleen. How dare you flaunt your money around?" Sean enunciated each word in a vicious, thick brogue. "She's thrilled with our recent agreement."

"Oh, am I now, Sean?" Kathleen stormed into the room, her face emanating pure outrage. By the looks of the two steps she'd walked, she'd been in the doorway for some time. The green ribbon tying back her silky hair was askew, and her dark eyes sparked with fury.

Rob's heart thumped in double time, his gaze riveted on her. He trod closer, intending to take her in his embrace. She shrugged him off and marched to within a foot of Sean.

"How are ya, luv?" Sean grinned.

"Luv? Luv? I never decided on any so-called agreement."

"You were earwigging?" Sean shoved his glass aside and rose to his feet. "Eavesdropping on a private chat?"

She stamped her foot. "This is *my* teahouse, not yours."

Her outburst earned her Sean's hangdog expression. "Kathleen, I beg your forgiveness. Just teasing. Obviously, you're a bundle of nerves with St. Paddy's looming. If you'll only—"

"Get out and don't come back."

"What? And go where—" he sputtered.

"Back to Boston, or Ireland. You've ruined it for yourself by your underhandedness." She shook her head and whispered, "I should've realized. Why do I never learn?"

Without so much as picking up his glass or bidding a courteous goodbye, Sean twisted on his heels and blustered through the front door with lengthy, purposeful strides.

"A sound good riddance to him," Rob said as the door slammed. "Now you and I can talk."

Whirling, her glare blasted fury. "As if I'm starving for a chat with you when you're always so preoccupied. I don't need you, and I don't need Sean."

"We've been separated for a while, but now I'm retired. Let's sit down and have a friendly discussion over a cup of tea. Candee mentioned you received an overdue bill for the gas convection oven. I can help by writing out—"

Kathleen's eyes widened, and tears erupted. "How can you be so brilliant and yet think you can buy me? I know what I want, and I can achieve it on my own."

"But I can fix this." He paused. He loathed saying the same words his father had used on him, and it hadn't resolved anything.

Inside his jacket pocket, his cell-phone rang.

She stepped behind a high-backed chair, as if fortifying herself against him. Deliberately, she unclasped the skeleton key locket from her neck and placed it on the chair.

He felt as if his heart was breaking. He rubbed his fist against his chest. His eyes blurred with the effort.

His phone kept ringing.

"Aren't you going to answer?" she asked.

"Later." He came forward and closed his hand over her shoulder. "It's not important."

More tears leaked from her eyes and rolled down her cheeks. He brushed them away, and she flinched.

"Rob, return to Miami where you obviously belong."

They were so close he could see the mix of emotions crossing her face—trembling chin, lips pressed together, the slight freckles dotting her wet cheeks.

"You must know how much I love you," he said.

She drew an inward breath. "Everyone seems to love me

these days." Despite her quaking voice, she remained perfectly still.

"I realize you're joking. I know how you Irish love to—"

"This Irishwoman is deadly serious." Her voice rose. "And another thing, which I'm certain will come as a shocking surprise to you: this business is mine, and mine alone."

CHAPTER 12

*A*t noon a day later, Kathleen sat in a high-backed chair in her teahouse and went through her text messages. Rob hadn't returned since their argument.

Instead, he'd called and left messages, saying he was staying at Candee and Teddy's home if she needed him.

Here's a final idea, he'd texted. *I've partnered with the Roses Chamber of Commerce for a ribbon-cutting ceremony on your official opening day. I know it's late but every bit of advertising helps.*

She hadn't responded.

I've done more market research and can set up a paid advertising media blitz which will coincide with St. Patrick's Day.

No. She'd set up all her online advertising ahead of time. She didn't need to lean on anyone except herself.

Why won't you let me help you? he'd asked again and again. *If you give us half a chance, you will remember how good we r together.*

That dart effectively pierced a nerve, and she'd closed her cell-phone and placed it in her purse.

A soft opening at the teahouse was arranged to begin at

four o'clock. This gave her and Nancy, the new employee, a chance to work out the crimps. Although the public was aware the teahouse was launching, Kathleen hadn't actively publicized it. Candee and Teddy sent their regards, as Joseph was participating in a horse show in Asheville and they couldn't attend. Keiran and Desiree were swamped at O'Malley's. And Sean had fled Roses.

Fortunately, another power outage hadn't occurred while customers dined later that evening, although the lock on the women's bathroom door broke.

Kathleen had also teamed up with Keiran and chalked his mushroom stroganoff as a main dinner entrée, quickly learning that serving the dish at five o'clock was too early and nine too late. Patrons preferred their dinner hour at seven, and she'd soon run out of mushroom stroganoff.

By nine p.m., the teahouse had emptied. After Nancy helped clean, she'd scanned a text message on her phone and departed without an explanation, forgetting her house keys in her haste. Because Nancy lived with her parents on the outskirts of Roses, Kathleen assumed she wouldn't need the keys until morning. Just in case, she put them aside near the herbal tea jars.

Kathleen dreaded the silence that enveloped the unoccupied rooms. It allowed her mind to dwell on all she'd lost. No longer could she hide behind work and busyness. She was forced to confront how much she missed Rob.

She slumped in the loveseat near the foyer and picked up her phone. She planned to make notes about the soft opening, tweaking her original vision. Despite her attempts, she couldn't focus, too intent on the honorable, caring man who had stolen her heart.

He'd been justifiably hurt and angry when he'd returned from Miami to find Sean lounging in her teahouse. And jealous, hiding his emotions by offering her money, hoping it would smooth the rift between them.

Her heart pinched. He'd worked for years to ensure a prosperous business, and desperately wanted her to succeed as well. He was the type of guy who helped people, soft-hearted and obliging. She knew he would never refuse her any favor. Rob was a man she could always count on.

He loved her. He'd told her so.

And what had she done when he'd proclaimed his love?

Why, she'd thrown it in his face.

"You must know how much I love you," he'd said.

"Everyone seems to love me these days," she'd responded coolly.

She read his numerous texts, pleading with her to give them a second chance.

She hadn't replied.

He had inquired about attending her soft opening.

I'd prefer you didn't. Please take my advice and stay in Miami.

And then he'd gone dark and hadn't contacted her since.

Dejectedly, she put her head in her hands and sobbed. Somehow, she'd done it again—succeeded in being involved in a heartbreaking romance with a man.

No. That wasn't true. Rob had given up his life in Miami, his thriving career, *everything* for her. And in the shared hours exploring a ghost town and dancing Irish jigs, amidst toppled tea cups and spilled vases filled with water and flowers, she'd fallen in love with him too.

Restless, she wiped her eyes, stood, and wandered through the vacant, lonely rooms, lighting night light candles and watering the potted green ferns.

Nothing was the same without him. The teahouse wasn't alive. He'd brought laughter, full of ideas, a ready smile on his face. And now he was gone.

She had driven him away, flatly refusing his help. She'd

seen the raw sadness in his blue eyes, the sagging around his mouth, when he'd said goodbye and walked out the door.

She leaned a shoulder on the windowpane and stared out at a cloudless night. Somewhere in the distance, a church bell pealed. When the time neared midnight, she sighted the star-shaped Big Dipper above the northern horizon.

Half-heartedly, she murmured, "Rob, how can you be so quiet after I told you to return to Miami? Did you forget me already?"

With a tattered sigh, she retreated to the back room and burrowed through the chest of drawers. She extracted the skeleton key locket and glided her fingers over the elaborate floral design. He'd confessed she held the key to his heart and requested she wear it always.

"Rainbows are brilliant in America too, Kathleen. And Roses is your new home."

And then the words that had dangled between them.

Here. With me.

She secured the locket, feeling better when it was near her heart, where it belonged.

With trembling hands, she texted him. If he accepted her apology and boarded a plane from Miami in the morning, he might arrive in Roses by midday. There was so much she needed to tell him. She'd been hurt by men countless times in her life and had been afraid to trust again. To love again.

But what was the world without love?

A FEW MINUTES after midnight brought a ping to Rob's cellphone. He'd been sitting by the guest bedroom's window in Candee's home, gazing idly outside at the familiar Big Dipper. The house was quiet, as the family was attending a horse show in Asheville.

"It better not be another manager texting me at this hour," he muttered, yanking the phone from his pocket.

Kathleen's caller ID appeared on the screen.

I miss you. Would you consider flying back from Miami?

And then: *1-800-IRELAND.*

He couldn't contain his excitement. He was already on his feet, his heart pounding with joy.

The drive to Kathleen's teahouse, which normally took under ten minutes, he covered in less than five. He didn't know what he'd say, wasn't sure how she'd respond. All that mattered was she had reached out to him and he was able to see her again.

He knocked once, hesitating only a second outside the teahouse's door, feeling the cool nip in the night air against his heated cheeks. Realizing the door was unlocked, he stepped inside. The tinkling bell announced his arrival.

She sat on a velvet loveseat in the foyer, her back to him, peering at a lengthy list. He recognized the business plan they'd drawn up together.

"Nancy?" Kathleen inquired without glancing up. "I put your keys aside for you. You'll see them by the tea jars on the counter."

He longed to rush to her, to pull her into his arms. She looked vulnerable, her red-gold hair shining in the delicate candlelight. Twice, he'd left her alone when he'd flown to Miami.

"Kathleen," he said.

She twisted and flew to her feet. "Rob?" All color drained from her complexion. "You're here? How?"

"I never left Roses."

"I thought you were in Miami."

"I couldn't leave." He strode to a cell-phone container and slipped his phone inside. "Our life together wasn't finished. It hadn't even started."

She moistened her lips, raced to him, and looped her arms around his neck.

He cradled her and guided her to the loveseat. She wore his locket over a starched white shirt and tailored black pants —the uniform she'd decided on for the teahouse. He traced his fingers along her high cheekbones. Her long dark lashes fluttered.

"I wish you'd been here, for the soft opening," she said.

"I wanted to. I'm here now. How did it go?"

"A few tweaks. Actually more than a few." She snuggled nearer his chest. "I learned people in Roses like to eat dinner at seven o'clock and be home early. The place cleared out by nine."

His lips brushed her forehead. "That's what a little bird told me."

She gazed up at him, this beauty he'd almost lost. "Who?" she asked.

"Nancy."

"My new employee?"

"Lovely woman, and absolutely exceptional. Sorry she'll no longer be working for you."

Rapidly, Kathleen blinked. "Excuse me?"

"Nancy will be working for me. Or rather, for us."

"You can't just walk in and steal my best employee."

"*Our* best employee."

"I'm not following." She frowned, her voice uncertain. "I finally …"

He pressed a finger to her mouth. "I bought another place. A ghost town, actually."

"You bought …" Incredulous, she stared at him. "You bought Hollan Farms? Now you'll be busier than ever."

"I didn't buy the town for me." He kissed her lips, softly, sweetly. "I bought the town for David to manage. I'm a silent investor."

She grinned, her face lighting with laughter. "The cow guy?"

"The one and only. And Nancy will help him." Rob twirled a lock of Kathleen's silky hair around his fingers. "Those two are young and ambitious. Hey, maybe it's the start of a budding romance. And you and I can oversee their progress once in a while."

"What will you do in the meantime?" she asked.

"I'm retired." He grinned. "But I'll be around, just in case you need my assistance."

"I do." She sat straighter, meeting his gaze with her own. "And I finally realized that accepting help isn't a sign of weakness, but of strength."

"You'll be far more able to reach your goals."

"Aye. So I've learned."

"Since you're so agreeable," he stood, then got down on one knee. "Will you marry an American man like me?"

"This is really happening," she murmured. "And my answer is, aye. Yes."

His smile reached his ears, and he went back to cuddling her on the loveseat. "After St. Patrick's Day, we'll look for a home in Roses," he said.

"I like the mild weather here. In Ireland, the days get dark quickly in the winter, and it's rainy and cold."

"In Miami, it's too hot most of the year."

Her deep brown eyes brimmed with tears. "Then Roses is perfect." She snuggled into his arms as his lips moved over hers.

"I love you more than anyone in the world," he whispered. "When you told me to leave, I vowed to wait however long it might take. I knew we had something extraordinary together."

"I've always wanted to visit Miami."

"I've always wanted to visit Ireland. I even have their toll-free number."

She laughed. "You don't really think that if you punch in 1-800-IRELAND, someone from Ireland will answer?"

With aching tenderness, he said, "I believe she will."

"I love you," she whispered.

"And I love you."

In the container by a table, his cell-phone rang.

She grinned up at him. "Ireland calling?"

"Toll-free."

"Aren't you going to answer it?"

"Nope. She's already answered all my dreams." He gazed around her comfortable teahouse, then at the exquisite woman in his arms.

A forever love.

THE END

RECIPE FOR AUNTIE PEGGY'S
IRISH BROWN BREAD

6 cups seedless raisins
  2 cups raisin water. Save after cooking the raisins

Cover the raisins with water. Cook until tender. Drain but SAVE two cups of the liquid after cooking.

DRY
    7 cups sifted, all-purpose flour
    1 teaspoon allspice
    4 teaspoons cinnamon
    2 teaspoons nutmeg
    4 teaspoons baking soda

WET
    1 cup butter, softened/room temperature
    3 cups sugar. Quantity is adjustable
    6 large eggs, room temperature.

IF YOU WISH, set aside the raisin water that is left and freeze it. Use it the next time you cook the raisins. Then, reduce the sugar by a cup. If using fewer than six cups of raisins to start with, reduce the sugar.

ALL INGREDIENTS SHOULD BE at room temperature.

Sift together all the dry ingredients in a large bowl and set aside.

Blend the butter, sugar and eggs. (I like to use the KitchenAid mixer for this step.)

Add the 2 cups of raisin liquid to the wet ingredients and mix well.

Add the wet mixture to the dry mix.

Stir in the 6 cups of cooked raisins and blend well.

Pour into four greased loaf pans. Bake for 1 to 1.25 hours at 325 degrees.

The top will spring back when touched lightly or a toothpick/cake tester works.

Enjoy!

A NOTE FROM JOSIE

Dear Friends,

Thank you for reading *1-800-IRELAND.* I hope you enjoyed it. This the third book in my contemporary sweet romance series: *Flipping for You.*

In this story, the 1-800 series continues in the charming town of Roses, North Carolina.

In 1-800-IRELAND, I gave Kathleen, from Oh Danny Boy, her own story. And, because Rob is a reader favorite from previous 1-800 books, I decided to give him his own book.

If you loved this sweet romance as much as I loved writing it, please help other people find *1-800-IRELAND* by posting your amazing review, as well as for the bundle: Irish Hearts

1-800-IRELAND is available in ebook, paperback, Large Print paperback, Hardcover, and audiobook.

My Spotify Play List for 1-800-IRELAND is here.

Want more Irish romances?

Irish Hearts

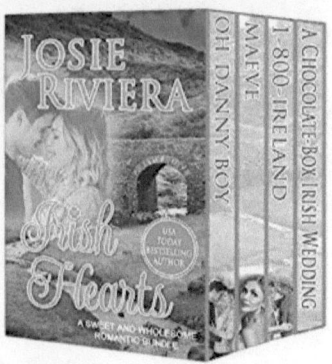

4 sweet romances in 1 bundle

USA TODAY BEST-SELLING AUTHOR

JOSIE RIVIERA

a Chocolate-Box

Irish Wedding

CHAPTER 1

*C*olum O' Brien didn't believe in Ireland's much-heralded mythology. Aye, he was Irish to the core, but there wasn't a wee bit of truth to mischievous leprechauns guarding pots of gold. Gold buried by fairies, no less. Goaded by skeptical amusement, he shook his head. He didn't put much stock in ancient Irish folklore.

Which led him to another thought: Dreams. Did they mean anything?

In any event, he wasn't looking forward to sleeping in his childhood bedroom tonight. He wondered if he'd have the same dream that had plagued him for months on end.

Over and over, just before waking, he'd gotten lost while driving on a shadowy, winding road, never finding his destination no matter how hard he tried.

Well, that assuredly wouldn't happen on this trip.

With a dismissive smile, he switched on the car radio, humming along to the folksy acoustics of "Wild Mountain Thyme," a Scottish tune.

The weather proved fine and clear for an Irish December afternoon, soon to glow with the dregs of sunset before the sky turned blue black. He opened the car window a crack, inhaling the earthy fragrance of peat smoke mingling with the bracing air of the Irish Sea. He flicked a glance toward the neighboring hills, marveling at the flicker of twinkling white lights in cottage windows—heralding the holiday season—then returned his focus to the zigzag coastal road.

A sign noted the final turnoff to a precarious, narrow two-lane road. Soon, he'd reach his family homestead in Wexford.

Thirty years ago, Colum could have accomplished this drive from his former Dublin ballet studio with one eye closed, but not anymore. His fifty-year-old eyes didn't see as well as they once did.

Unexpectedly, heavy clouds began lowering over the surrounding hay pastures. Rain spattered his windshield.

He slowed his speed. It was as if he'd driven off into a different country with no recognizable landmarks. The sudden storm had even shut off his GPS.

Where was he?

The mist thickened. Road signs became unreadable. He lowered the volume on the radio.

Instinct told him he must be nearing the last tiny village on the outskirts of Wexford. Thankfully, the taillights of another car appeared ahead.

Perhaps a long-lost relative?

Colum's widowed father had insisted on a gathering at his seaside home for his wedding celebration and asked Colum to be the best man. His father was marrying a dear friend and set a December wedding.

At first, Colum had made excuses for not attending; he taught numerous dance classes, plus was helping Sean, a troubled young man in his twenties. Years earlier, he'd met the lad at a volunteer performance in Dublin. A feature story by an American newsman, Patrick Gervez, had spotlighted how Colum's ballet troupe had given back to the city by inviting underprivileged teens to watch free productions. Since then, he'd claimed Sean as his nephew, relocated him to Farthing, and helped whenever possible.

Thus, it was difficult to get away.

This trip was an eleventh-hour decision. Not that Colum didn't love his father—though in truth, he'd been resistant to return to Wexford. The longer time passed, the more he'd lost touch with his hometown. And whenever he drove these roads, his heart remembered Keira, his high school sweetheart.

Now it was her mother who would be his father's bride.

Would Keira be there? Wexford was the last place Colum had seen her several decades earlier. But no, she lived in London now, and his father would have mentioned her attending the wedding.

Perhaps. Perhaps not. He and his father didn't converse much.

The car ahead accelerated around a sharp curve, slid off the main road, then skidded to a stop on a gravel lane.

Colum's heartbeat slowed, his fingers tightened on the steering wheel. He stomped on the brakes and swerved onto the shoulder. Quickly shutting off the engine, he dashed from his car.

As suddenly as it started, the rain quit. The clouds thinned; then slunk away.

He dragged in a breath as the driver stepped out of the car.

A woman. A fair-skinned, willowy woman. And with her came a whisper of a memory: Their shared childhood and his love for her.

"Are you all right?" Anxiety brought a tremor to his voice. Fresh breezes cooled his heated cheeks.

"I'm brilliant." She peered at him with keen blue eyes.

Blond hair, threaded with silver, tumbled down her back. The ends were tipped in . . . pink?

"Colum O'Brien. Is that you?" She touched a hand to her full, inviting lips—lips he well remembered.

He froze, his gaze fixed on her. He couldn't reply.

Keira Murphy. Here. He'd never expected to see her again.

"Aye. It's me." He strode closer; a tongue-tied moment.

She offered that same heart-shattering smile he'd thought about for decades.

"I'm delighted to see you, my long-lost friend," she said.

He couldn't stop gazing at her—her vivid blue eyes, sooty-black lashes and lovely slim figure. There were so many things he wanted to say, so many times he'd longed to hear her voice again.

"I'm happy to see you too." He cleared his throat. "You look grand."

More than grand. She looked exquisite.

He took both her hands in his and kissed her, a fleeting, polite brush of his lips on her cheek. Casual, yet intimate.

Her hair smelled like lilies, her skin soft and silky.

She breathed in a slight inhale, then pulled away.

He drew a shaky breath and ordered himself not to question why he'd been reduced to a long-lost friend status when they'd shared so much more.

Without another word, she moved to her car, her motions graceful. He held open the door for her and ensured she was settled. Then he headed back to his car and followed her to Wexford.

CHAPTER 2

The following morning, Keira sat in an oversized Adirondack chair on the O'Brien's spacious lawn. Moss grew on the weathered walls of the house, and the thatched roof drooped at the eaves. A string of holiday lights wound around each window, a cheerful reminder of the upcoming festivities. The scent of dew hung in the air, the grass damp from an earlier rain.

She regarded the stone markings at the front of the O'Brien property, the adjacent fields dotted by sheep, the sparkling waters of the Irish Sea.

"Hello, Keira," a deep voice called. Colum came from behind, covered her eyes with his hands, then immediately removed them. "Guess who?"

Her stomach fluttered, and she bit down on her lips to hide her smile. She admired his easy-going walk as he stepped around to face her. He was a man comfortable in his own skin, whereas she considered herself too tall and ungainly.

"That was easy," she teased. "You could've given me another minute to guess."

"I assumed you'd know it was me right away." He grinned. "May I begin our day by complimenting you, because you are gorgeous?"

"Thank you." She'd dressed in jeans and a red wool sweater, and twisted her hair back into a casual bun. She'd fussed with her appearance in anticipation of seeing him. "Were you comfortable sleeping in your childhood bedroom again?" she asked.

"The sea air is a balm. Without fail, I sleep well in Wexford." He dropped into the chair beside her and yanked out a cigarette. "It's a surprise, aye?"

"The fact you're still smoking? You vowed to quit when you were a teen."

"Over three decades later, and I constantly try to quit, although it's obvious I'm unsuccessful." He granted a rueful smile. "You never liked it."

"Still don't."

"I defer to your wishes, then." He slipped the cigarette back into his pocket, then rolled up the sleeves of his jean jacket.

"How can you dance and do that to your lungs?" As he smirked at her response, she studied him. His arms were athletic and muscular, his physique toned and fit in slim-fitting black pants and a grey knit sweater. She remembered when he'd held her at this very spot, on a similar breezy morning—a few days before she'd departed for London—a few days before New Year's Eve.

She shifted her gaze to the water. "So what's a surprise?"

"Your mum is marrying my dad," he said. "A gala event to begin the holidays."

"The best time of the year."

"Christmas?"

"And New Year's," she replied. "In fact, the entire month of December."

"The season isn't special for me . . . although I'm thankful for the adorable children I teach. The look on their faces is priceless because they're so excited."

She gestured to the O'Brien's home. The natural holly wreath hung on the back door. "We used to leave sacks by the fireplace on Christmas Eve, remember?"

"In the hopes the sacks would be filled with toys on Christmas Day." He chuckled. "Then we'd set out milk and bread on the kitchen table."

"In our house, we'd opt for a pint of Guinness and mince pies." She sighed, the memories poignant. "My mum has been alone since my father died."

"Similarly for my dad when my mum passed away."

"I recall that day." Keira had searched for Colum and discovered him sitting by the shore, his arms around his knees, his face wet with tears. At fourteen years old he'd been embarrassed she'd found him crying, for he despised weakness in himself. His shoulders were drooped, and his voice a whisper, but he'd finally relented and invited her to stay. In return, she'd offered consolation and her undying loyalty.

"Boys don't cry," he'd stated.

"But men do," she'd assured. *"Real men aren't ashamed to shed tears and show their emotions."*

"Our parents have been friends for years," Colum was saying.

"Like us." She folded her lips together. Why had she spoken the words aloud?

Until you left.

Colum hadn't uttered a sound, but, judging from his tightened expression, she could read his thoughts. They'd been inseparable. That's what happened when you were next-door neighbors.

She fingered the sleeves of her sweater. "I realize my departure from Wexford was sudden."

He shrugged.

"You know why." Too edgy to sit still, she shifted. "There were goals I wanted to accomplish before we settled down."

"Shall we give it a name?" he asked.

"What?" She sat straighter. "Me leaving?"

"Let's call it the demise of a friendship."

She flinched, as if his statement was a physical blow, even more so because of the slight catch in his tone. He'd been hurt.

For years, they'd planned to attend the same university in a neighboring town. That had only taken place for one semester. They'd pledged to stay in touch, although the busyness of life had taken hold.

"I said I would wait for you." His voice was quiet and solemn. "However, it was you who declared that we were young and couldn't plan our lives around a final commitment."

"Not once did you demand that I abandon my dreams."

"I wanted you to ride your rising career to the top," he said. "I never would've taken your achievements away."

Why? Did he love her so much that her happiness was more important than his?

She waited for him to say more. When he didn't, she searched his handsome face, although his features were remarkably bland. "You accomplished your dream," she finally said.

"Which dream was that?"

"Dancing professionally. You lifted those ballerinas effortlessly into the air. How many dancers can claim that?"

"All credited to thousands of hours of rehearsals; and workouts." He quirked a silvery-grey eyebrow. "Did you ever attend any of my performances?"

"No, not live, but I discovered YouTube."

He looked pleased. Something stirred in the fathomless depths of his green eyes, and her heart rate doubled.

"You watched clips?" he inquired.

"Aye."

More than clips. She'd watched his full performances.

"And you?" He shoved his hands into his pockets. "Did you find what you were looking for?"

"For a while, until I grew too old to model."

"You're not old."

"High fashion modeling is extremely competitive." The wind pushed her hair back. "When I was awarded a generous contract from an exclusive agency, I couldn't turn it down."

"And off to England you went. You hightailed it out of here before the New Year's bells rang."

She should've felt cornered by his statement—defensive. But this was Colum. She'd known him since they were children. She knew his nature. He was her constant companion, and she'd confided everything to him.

"You're asking me to apologize?" She fixed him with a level gaze. "I did on numerous occasions. How could I start our life in Wexford when London beckoned?"

"True." He watched the sea, and she followed his stare. The water was calm, the salty breeze conjuring images of picnics—wicker hampers stuffed with sausage sandwiches, sliced apples, and spice cake—while herring gulls squawked overhead.

"Fame and fortune, Kiki," he said. "Both are heady sensations."

Kiki. Her cheeks warmed. She'd nearly forgotten his nickname for her.

"I craved more." She swallowed and lifted her chin. "The excitement of a sizable city and glamorous occupation. Wexford is . . ."

He swept out his hands. "Adorable."

"You didn't stick around, either," she pointed out.

"No reason to."

Because of her? She pondered whether she should ask him. She didn't.

"I never congratulated you on your success," he went on. "Or rather, I did, but you didn't respond."

"I'm sorry. I was wrong not to answer your letters." Those precious letters—every word had broken her heart—but she couldn't write back, it would have only broken *his* heart. She'd established a new world—so different from his in only a matter of months. Nonetheless, his letters had slid from her fingers as she'd sat in her tiny London flat and wept. Joy to hear from him, bittersweet longing for leaving him behind, and the injustice of a demanding career that had initiated their separation.

She sighed. "My work was exhausting, and I hardly had a moment to breathe."

He greeted her explanation with a quick nod.

They'd been best friends. No. More than that. They'd been first loves.

"I'm standing up in the wedding." Keira navigated to a safer subject and offered a modest bow. "I'm the matron of honor."

"I'm the best man."

"Your father spoke of your obligations in Farthing," she said. "I wasn't expecting to see you."

Colum's occasional trips to Wexford over the years never had seemed to correspond with hers.

"Sean, a young lad who is like a nephew to me, continually needs my help," Colum replied. "I met him through Patrick Gervez, an American newsman who traveled to Dublin to feature a story on an outreach ballet program. Nowadays, Sean's graphic design business is doing fairly well, and he moved into his own flat. I packed his fridge with food, a matter of great importance to a twenty-something."

Typical Colum, she reflected. Forever helping people whenever possible.

"Is Sean independent?" she asked.

"He's getting there." Colum pulled his hands from his pockets and stared down at them. "I worry for him, though. I want him to be successful."

"I remember how you repeatedly volunteered at the homeless shelter in town and then organized plays for the children. You gave graciously of your expertise and talents."

"I tried."

"Help Sean, but don't give him handouts."

He grinned. "Advice now, Keira?"

"I speak from experience as a mother of two adult daughters who are often headstrong. I continued to indulge them for years, which was a mistake." She ran a hand through her hair. "Do you own a home in Farthing?"

"Renting is better for me," Colum replied. "My savings are stable, although I'm not wealthy."

"I just bought my own place."

"Congratulations! Where?"

"Take a glance to your right."

He turned. "Your mum's grand cottage?"

"She's moving in with your dad after the wedding, so, I figured, why not? It's my childhood home. Plus, I'm here to care for our parents as they age."

He leaned toward her and gave a heavy nod. "Aging is definitely a fact of everyday life, and it will be a comfort for them to have you next door."

"Their well-being is important, both physical and emotional."

"Aye." He shot a rueful grin. "And convenient when you need a cup of sugar."

"I don't bake." Keira beamed. "I sew."

"Right. How could I forget?" Colum offered a bemused chuckle. "I rang my father about my change of plans—before he requested someone else to be the best man."

"Who would he ask?"

"A cousin, maybe. Can't think of anyone who is suitable, though."

"You work in Farthing?" She'd already asked too many questions. She had at least a dozen more. She was so comfortable, so at ease conversing with him.

"I'm an instructor at Miss Clara's School of Dance," he replied. "Primarily, I teach preschoolers, and I love that age."

"Sweet ages."

"Someday, I fancy directing a public theater for adults and children."

"Underprivileged?"

"Aye, and also open to anyone in the community."

"In Farthing?"

"I haven't decided."

"You never married," she said. "Never had children."

"My longest relationship lasted all of eight months. I wasn't a particularly attentive partner while I concentrated on my career." With a noncommittal nod, he added, "Wexford was abuzz when you wed your agent in London. You were only twenty at the time."

"Henry was several years older."

"By two decades," Colum corrected. "A sophisticated man, I assume?"

Her face heated with the pain of the recollection. "He introduced me to a glittery circle. I thought of you when I met his friends at posh parties. We would've had a laugh at their uppity airs."

He grinned and leaned closer. "And your daughters are now . . ."

"Almost thirty."

"I always wanted children," he said.

"Twin daughters?"

"One would've been fine." His tone softened. "Two are better."

"Yet you never married . . ." Keira stammered with her response. When Colum studied her with those mesmerizing eyes, she forgot all rational thought. "You'll meet my girls. They're flying in from London. They'll miss the ceremony because of work, but will stay for a while afterwards."

"Through Christmas and New Year's?"

"They both have significant others in London, so I doubt it."

"I'm leaving a couple days after the service. I'm teaching several dance classes, then overseeing a holiday recital for the little ones after Christmas. The students have been preparing for months."

"You'll miss Christmas in Wexford, then. I hope to decorate my shop and my new home as soon as our parents are wed." Her brows knitted. "Will you return for New Year's?"

"Perhaps." Assiduously, he avoided her gaze.

"Remember the fun we had on New Year's Eve?"

Gently, he touched her arm. "Our families would visit for nibbles and drinks."

"And beforehand, my mum would clean the house from top to bottom."

"'To signify a fresh start for the upcoming year."

"May I confess something?" she asked.

Colum automatically seemed to tense at her question. "Of course."

"On New Year's Eve, I placed a mistletoe under my pillow," she said.

"In the hopes of seeing your future partner in your

dreams." He peeked at her left hand. She'd taken her wedding band off years ago. "Is your husband . . .?"

"Henry and I divorced when our daughters finished primary school." Keira rubbed the back of her neck. "We only stayed in a polite agreement that long for the children's sake."

"Was it the right decision?"

"Each couple's choice is personal and involves many factors. From my experience, I should've left him sooner." Her marriage had been a slow deterioration of her self-confidence. As soon as her career had fallen to a standstill, Henry lost interest in her. He'd also worn away her independence and monitored her calories.

Colum glanced up and motioned toward the shore, extending a wave and a smile.

She followed his gaze to their parents. Cheryl and Richard, both in their late seventies, strolled arm and arm by the water's edge. Her mum wore a wide brimmed straw hat and billowy yellow-floral dress. Colum's father was stout and fit, as well as green-eyed, good-humored, and engaging. It gladdened Keira's heart to see their smiles. Love occurred at any age, she supposed. Just not for her.

She'd never been content in her marriage—even before Henry's verbal abuse. Had she been forever seeking the right man? She'd dated after her divorce, but no sparks.

Her chest filled with regret as she met Colum's gaze. He'd been her first love. Had he been her true love?

"Divine weather," he was saying.

"No rain in the forecast." She managed a radiant smile. "Let's hope the sun shines for the wedding."

"It's risky planning an outdoor ceremony in December," Colum noted.

"Wexford is considered the sunny southeast of Ireland. Besides, they're renting a tent with heaters for the reception. They can dash inside if need be."

"Good thing. There is constantly a threat of showers in an Irish forecast."

"Or a downpour," she inserted.

He stood and peered at the blue sky, the stretch of wispy white clouds. "Will you join me for a coffee in town? Just like we used to."

"When we were supposed to be in class."

"We'd have the craic—a good laugh and loads of fun." He chuckled. She remembered that chuckle—rich and pure and inviting. "We were a rascally pair,—ducking out of school early."

She held up a hand. "Speak for yourself."

"Hah! Half the time, you'd initiate our adventures. We'd pool our lunch money, hop on a bus, and eventually land at Michael D's whiling away the afternoon over scones and coffee and homework."

"Homework?"

He smiled. "Once in a while."

"I dine at Michael D's often."

His smile wavered. "I'm trying to get my head around the fact that all this time I assumed you still lived in London."

"I own a dressmaker's shop a few doors down from Michael D's," she explained. "In fact, I designed my mum's wedding dress. Care to take a peek?"

"Isn't it bad luck to see the bride's dress before the wedding?"

"Only if you're the groom." She accepted his extended hand and got to her feet. "Don't take any photos to show your dad."

"You're the one who could never keep a secret. Chatterbox."

She gave his shoulder a playful nudge as they began walking. "And you were quiet."

"So many memories." Conflicting emotions flashed across

his well-defined features—his sharp cheekbones that reminded her of a proud Roman warrior. His gaze locked with hers, a silent communication. He knew her so well. She'd never been at a loss for words, and they'd sit for hours. Colum, attentive and encouraging, while she chatted endlessly. She'd become a famous designer, and he'd continue volunteering and open a performing arts school. Perhaps they'd marry in the winter. A Christmas wedding, or New Year's . . .

Their lives had taken such different paths.

But what if . . .

No, no, no. She refused to play the "what if" game.

"What's the name of your shop?" Colum asked.

"Keira's Wexford Boutique."

They stepped onto a stone path, lingering to appreciate the buds of holly and pansies blooming up from the cold ground.

"You loved fashion." Colum paused to pick a bouquet, handing the flowers to her. "You made me a shirt once."

She sniffed, savoring the fragrant scent. He'd frequently slip her a spray of cowslip or clover or shamrocks—depending on the season.

"I sewed the shirt from jersey cotton fabric and a pre-made sewing pattern," she replied. "It was tight on you."

"I wore it often."

"Only so you wouldn't hurt my feelings."

He'd ignored teasing from the other boys and had worn her handmade shirt with pride. He constantly looked out for her. Her protector. He wanted to make her happy.

"You sewed this for me, Kiki?" he'd asked with a broad smile when she'd presented it to him. *"It's brilliant."*

He'd tugged it over his dog-eared t-shirt. He was tanned and muscular by then—on the cusp of adulthood—nearing eighteen.

The shirt hadn't been brilliant—an amateur's attempt at sewing and design—boasting a bold Hawaiian pattern of multicolored birds and leaves. Nevertheless, her interest in fashion, encouraged by Colum, had thrived.

"Is your shop successful?" He stood so close, the warmth of his skin heated her own. She inhaled the crisp scent of the sea. Knowing him, he'd probably gone for a swim at sunup.

He still had the muscular build of his younger self, his profile lithe, yet solid. His eyes were a mossy green—reminding her of the color of the forest after a hard rain. His hair was salt and pepper, raked short and side-swept.

"I'm happy," she acknowledged. "I've come to realize this idyllic wee town is my home. For me, happiness constitutes success."

"Ahh, living in Wexford."

She frowned. "Is there a problem?"

"Little towns are ideal for many chaps." He exhaled. "However, the country character here, coupled with my recollections of the old ways . . ."

"You find fault with our traditions? Our folklore?"

"Some of it. Nevertheless, a large city offers more theater and restaurant choices." He winked. "Plus, no one remembers me as an awkward adolescent."

"You were a pro in every sport. Whereas I—all legs and arms—"

CHAPTER 3

"*Y*ou're exquisitely perfect." Colum blurted the words before he could stop himself. He scanned Keira's delicate profile—the curve of her nose, her flawless complexion with a sprinkling of freckles, and heard the sincerity in her tone. She actually didn't realize how attractive she was.

However, her blue eyes shone with a spirit that hadn't been diminished by hardship.

Her youthful features had matured, fulfilling the certainty of loveliness, enriched with a mellowness that had developed with maturing. Her posture was straight, her figure slender.

His only desire was to touch her, kiss her, cherish the delightful feelings intensifying inside him—the first true emotions he'd felt in decades.

He cupped her cheek. "Numerous points in my life have reminded me of you. I wondered if our mutual memories ever caused you to smile."

He braced himself for her reply. When she finally dragged her gaze to his, she drew a wobbly breath. "I laughed a lot in London whenever I remembered our adventures."

He bent his head and his lips grazed hers. So delicious, so inviting. "You're my precious Kiki," he murmured. "You've been my forever—"

"No." She tugged free. Her complexion was flushed, her eyes wet. "You're leaving in a few days."

"Aye, but there's no reason why I can't return. I've never stopped thinking about you." He brushed the shiny hair from her forehead and grinned at the pink highlighted tips. In her teens she'd been the town nonconformist, experimenting with bizarre fashions. However, the bright makeup and outlandish feather hats had never diminished the beauty of her high cheekbones and expressive eyes. No wonder a London modeling agency had signed her on the spot.

"Words are easy, Colum." He respected the proud grace of her walk as she stepped away. "Circumstances may prevent a person from following through—no matter their intentions."

When they reached her driveway, Keira insisted on driving them to town, vowing to take the curves slowly in light of the previous evening's mishap. She didn't. If anything, she accelerated during the ten-minute drive, while he gripped the edge of the passenger seat. When they arrived at her shop, she rummaged in her handbag for the keys.

He squinted through the wavy glass window of the vacant building next door. The exterior paint flaked at random, the interior was dust-coated, the walls cracked.

"What business was here previously?" Colum asked.

"Nothing for years," she answered. "There was talk of converting the space into a high-class hotel, but the funds never came through."

She finally found the key, and they stepped inside her shop.

It was tidy and spotless, and scents of cedar and mint lingered in the air. Clothes racks sported fine woolens and tweeds, hand knit scarves and cable stitch cream sweaters tagged to sell.

"Do you employ a staff?" he asked.

"Recently, I hired a mother and her adult daughter. They're smart, efficient, and excellent seamstresses." Keira walked to a back room and brought out a knee-length lace dress in a champagne shade, along with a flowered crown headpiece. She illustrated how she'd sewn each delicate button by hand.

"Tasteful for your mum." He applauded. "May I ask what the daughter of the bride is wearing?"

Keira winked. "It's a surprise."

"In secondary school, I'd ask what you planned to wear the following day, and you'd consistently say—"

"It's a surprise," they chimed in unison.

"Why did you forever ask me the same question, Colum?"

"To prepare myself." He attempted to keep his features straight. "I never knew what newfangled outfit you'd come up with."

"Fashion is fun. An adventure."

He rolled his eyes. "You found enough for both of us." He'd willingly gone anywhere she'd dragged him and felt fortunate just to be with her.

"I wished to dress better than those pretty girls in school who flirted with you," she said.

He chucked her under the chin. "I believe you were jealous."

"Believe whatever suits you."

"Were you . . . jealous?" He drew her near, held her close. He couldn't help himself. His yearning for her slowed his breathing.

As he gazed into her eyes, the seconds paused—becoming the shared remembrances of delightful hours, of days, of years.

He'd sought to deny it, but he'd never been able to resist her. When they were young, they'd fallen into an easy friendship—enjoyable and uncomplicated. By their teens, their relationship had changed. Romance began to bloom—although they'd both resisted the attraction to each other.

For decades afterward, his thoughts had gravitated toward her. How was she faring in London? Had she forgotten him? Undoubtedly, because she was married.

But now they were reunited, and the seasons apart were a mere moment in time.

"Jealous? Don't be ridiculous. You flatter yourself." Keira fussed with a tweed cape on a hanger, fumbling with the fabric. "The programs you choreographed at the Wexford homeless shelter were fun and uplifting, and you were only in your teens."

"Thank you. I love working with children." He wanted to congratulate her on navigating the subject change so seamlessly.

She turned toward him. "Do you still dance and perform?"

"There aren't many roles for fifty-something males," he replied.

"You were a key dancer with the Dublin ballet."

"Until I reached thirty. Then the younger, ambitious men were happy to replace me."

"Same in my occupation." She went back to fussing with the cape. "Runway models are most successful between the ages of sixteen and twenty-one."

"And afterwards?"

"I did catalogues. And sewing to make ends meet while raising two daughters."

"You're exceptional, Kiki. You lived on your own in London."

Tears welled in her eyes. He didn't expect them.

"My ex-husband, Henry, considered me obsolete when I aged out of working the runway." The cape fell off the hanger. She bent to pick it up. "After our divorce, I continued to question my self-worth."

"Did he abuse you?

"Not physically. His abuse was emotional." She lifted her hands, then let them drop. "I should've divorced him sooner, but I was trapped. Two young daughters and no way to support us."

"Now you're successful and content."

"I am." She laughed, unforced and laid-back. "This tiny slice of the world is my lifeline, and I'm not relocating anytime soon."

Life in a microscopic town was ideal for some people, just not for him. He dismissed the unspoken thought and sought a more manageable topic. Absently, he fingered a velvet hanger, while he relished spending the day with her. Finally, the Keira he recognized was emerging from behind her careful wall. Honestly explaining her hardships, without sugarcoating what he'd imagined had been her opulent London lifestyle.

"Ready to lead the way to Michael D's?" he suggested.

"Considering the coffee shop is a few doors down, it's not difficult."

"Do they still serve tea cakes?"

"Aye. And buttered scones with strawberry jam. Your favorite. The new owner kept the same menu."

He patted his stomach. "Your mum baked superb scones with lemon curd and whipped cream. You brought them to me after my ballet practice, rolled up in foil and topped with a silver bow."

"She still bakes over a turf fire. Batches of soda bread sit on our kitchen counter as I speak."

"Thus a delightful afternoon awaits."

She narrowed her gaze. "Colum O'Brien, you can't sample desserts and bread all day."

"Watch me." He laced his fingers through hers and led her out of the shop.

They passed McKay's jewelers and peered through the display case window. As was customary in many of Ireland's shops, the Claddagh Ring took center stage.

"Love, loyalty, and friendship." Keira admired an array of sterling silver and gold bands.

"Did your mum hand her wedding ring down to you?"

"I married in London, and she didn't attend because my father was sick. He died a year later, and she continued to wear the ring on her right hand. Now that she's marrying your father, she placed it in her bedroom drawer for safe-keeping."

Colum hooked his arm around her shoulders. "Awaiting you."

"I won't marry again."

"Why ever not?" he asked.

"Once was enough. I'm obviously not good at marriage." Her tone thickened, and she clasped her hands together. "Perhaps one of my daughters will wear it someday."

He swallowed the dull ache in his throat. He could still visualize Keira planning their future all those years ago.

And after we graduate from university, Colum, we'll marry, she'd declared. Her color was high, her joy bubbling and infectious. *Won't it be grand?*

"Aye." He'd cradled her in his arms. *"Grand, indeed."*

CHAPTER 4

When they reached the O'Brien's cottage, Keira invited Colum into her home. The comforting scent of buttermilk and raisins and freshly baked Irish soda bread greeted him as they entered the light-filled kitchen. The walls were painted a dove gray, and a bold patterned rug covered the ancient tiled floor. Photographs littered a side bureau. Several were black and white photos of him and Keira. In one, they stood by the shore. He displayed a wiggling fish—their only catch that day—while she beamed, her light-blond hair in a long braid over her shoulder, and proudly held up the fishing pole. They were eight years old.

Keira gestured to the loaves stacked beneath numerous glass containers. "All ready for the reception."

"Your mum shouldn't bake for her own wedding."

"Why not? Baking is therapy."

He lifted a lid. "May I?"

"Sure. I'll slice a loaf and brew a pot of tea."

A few minutes later, she poured two steaming cups of robust breakfast tea and combined loads of milk and sugar into her cup. Once she settled, he seated across from her. The expansive bay window boasted an unobstructed view of the craggy hills and sea beyond.

"Thus, our parents are out and about today," he said.

"They drove to Waterford." Keira set the white porcelain teapot on the table. "My mum wished to speak with the DJ in person."

Colum sat back in joking amazement. "No bagpipes tomorrow?"

"The piper will perform when guests arrive and leave the ceremony." She sipped her tea and gazed at him over the rim of her cup. "At the reception, she insists on traditional Irish folk music."

Colum lifted his teacup in a salute. "She is a wise woman."

"I agree. She allowed me to make my own mistakes." Keira poured more tea. "The rehearsal begins in a couple hours, and the pastor arrives at five o'clock."

"What rehearsal?"

"We'll practice walking in and out, and where we'll stand during the ceremony. Didn't your father mention anything?"

Colum drummed his fingers on the wooden table. "Men don't talk much."

"My mum requested that you and I plan an impromptu party for afterwards."

"Did she now?" he asked. "I could do with more warning."

"Are you busy?"

"Not at all."

"Good." Keira smiled. She was gorgeous when she smiled. Her face was all gentle curves, her silky hair tumbling over her shoulders. "I'll ring a few places in town."

She made quick work of the arrangements, then picked up their tea cups and placed them in the sink. After she finished, she remained silent for a beat.

"When, exactly, do you return to Farthing?" she inquired.

The anticipation of a commitment was unmistakable. The

speculation of "what If" he didn't have to leave.

But he did. He'd created another life. He leased a flat and had resided in Farthing for ages.

He traced his fingers along the sides of her face and smoothed back her blond hair. She turned her cheek nearer his palm before she slipped away.

Did his remembrances of their former years—when they'd finished each other's sentences—bring her the same pangs of heartfelt longing? He'd presumed his reminiscences were embellished by the idealism of youth. Now he wasn't so sure.

"My preschoolers await my return," he said.

"Do you enjoy teaching the younger age group?"

"Absolutely. I use distraction and positive feedback. And I heap on the compliments when the children point their toes."

"Do they . . . point their toes?"

"Hardly ever." He grinned as she laughed out loud.

Keira's radiance brightened his mood. When he'd lost his mum, he'd wept, his sorrow unbearable. Keira had been there —quietly consoling, encouraging him to express his grief. She'd put aside her sewing that day, changed her plans. Comrades till the end, they'd vowed. They'd sat tight for hours until the sky darkened.

He was her priority, she'd assured him. As she'd been his.

"My American friends, Patrick and Cora Gervez, have flown to Ireland for a holiday," Colum continued. "He's the newsman who introduced me to Sean in Dublin. In any case, I want to show him and his wife, Cora, around Farthing. As soon as the recital is over, I'll return to Wexford."

"Is that a promise?"

"A promise and then some." He kissed her temple. "That is, unless you're traveling somewhere for New Year's Eve?"

"Have you forgotten, Colum?" Lightly, she stroked his hand. Or maybe he stroked hers. "I'm not going anywhere."

CHAPTER 5

*A*lthough rehearsal dinners in Ireland weren't standard, Keira opted for a casual soiree with hors d'oeuvres, oysters, and pints of beer at sunset. They arranged tables and chairs under a canopied pergola on the sandy beach, and Colum and his father built a smoldering bonfire between the sand dunes. The fire whispered hisses, the flames flickering, and the air smelled of smoke and pine.

Bottles of water were plentiful, along with a marble board laden with a wheel of moist blue cheese, sharp cheddar, goat's cheese, soda crackers and crusty baguettes.

Keira reached for a handful of grapes as she admired the blade-leaf potted plants adorning the tables. The men had secured strings of subdued vintage light bulbs to the pergola.

Colum came to stand beside her, his arm brushing hers. He wore slim-fitting swimming trunks and a striped polo shirt, and his smile enhanced his good-looking face.

"May I?" he asked.

"May you what?" Her chest surged with excitement. She couldn't refute the unmistakable magnetism whenever he neared, as if an electrical arc sizzled between them.

He touched a finger to his bottom lip, a teasing gesture she fondly recalled. "May I have your grapes?"

"There's plenty where these came from, and I can assure they're all the same." She motioned toward the tables. "We requested the caterer bring fresh figs and dried apricots too. Remember?"

"You did most of the arranging."

"Correction. *All* the arranging."

"Right." Her remark earned a chuckle. "Well, I'd prefer your grapes."

"You constantly stole my food when we were young."

He swept an arm around her waist. "Not stealing. I asked first."

With an exaggerated sigh, she handed him the grapes. "Help yourself."

"I'd like nothing better than to help myself . . . to a kiss." His soft breath brushed her cheek. His green eyes smoldered as he bent his head and pressed his lips on hers.

The kiss deepened, and she wound her hands around his shoulders.

Somewhere near the house, her mum called. Colum broke the kiss, and an unexpected loneliness filled Keira's heart. With a sigh, she encouraged herself to yield to reason. Too many years had passed. Was it too late to start their romance again—simply pick up where they left off?

A possibility. But life, she'd discovered, was seldom simple. Twists and turns were encountered around every bend.

She plucked his arm from her waist and turned. "We're coming, mum," she called back.

Colum held her hand as they started toward the house. "I always admired your generous nature," he said.

"As if I had a choice," she joked.

He polished off her entire sprig of grapes and they shared a laugh.

He had laugh lines now. So did she.

As they walked, she reflected on their day. She liked sitting at the kitchen table with him and planning a rehearsal dinner celebration. She liked everything about this charming man with rock solid arms and sturdy shoulders.

"My two favorite young people," her mum declared when Keira and Colum approached. "You make a stunning couple."

"We're hardly a couple," Keira replied. "And we're hardly young."

Colum's father strode over. "Could've fooled me on both counts."

Their smiling approval was so contagious that Keira couldn't curb her grin.

"Your mum and my father are wise." Colum followed his declaration with a throaty laugh. She glanced at him, startled to see the love shining in his eyes, and her heart soared.

After chatting about the wedding and wishing their parents "good night," Colum kept his fingers firmly around Keira's and led her to the waterfront.

Those who chose to swim after the rehearsal had been encouraged to wear their swimsuits, and Keira had arranged a basket of towels on the beach. The full moon rose, a deep silver disc, steady and true, much like the fine-looking man smiling down at her.

Colum gestured with his chin. "Lots of folks are enjoying the water this evening. Are you up for a swim?"

"They're mental. The sea is freezing."

He chuckled. "It'll get even colder in January."

She pointed to the waves slicing across the rocks. "Is your judgement clouded? Have you been drinking?

"I don't drink alcohol."

She knew that about him. He'd never changed.

A sparkle lit his eyes. "We Irish are a hardy people."

"Uh, huh."

"Invariably, I swam faster once we reached our teens."

"Invariably?" She placed her hands on her hips, her legs slightly apart. "Is your fancy word a dare?"

"Absolutely." He shrugged off his shirt. His chest was firm and well-defined. Graceful and compelling. A man who devoted his life striving for beauty and artistry.

"As you may recall," she said, "I'm an exceptional swimmer."

"You should be." Wryly, he grinned. "You live by the sea."

She bumped up against him. "So did you." She untied her white shimmer lace coverup and set it on a chair. Her vivid-purple swimsuit sported a sweetheart neckline and revealed a peek of fair skin.

His admiring stare wasn't lost on her and her cheeks heated.

He grabbed her hand, and they dashed into the frigid water—the spray soaking their faces. Total immersion brought her teeth to chattering within minutes. They splashed each other before Keira admitted defeat and they headed for shore.

Colum snatched several thick towels and wrapped one around her. He arranged another on the sand close to the bonfire and beckoned her to sit.

With a lightness in her limbs, she obliged.

He sat beside her, tucked the towel nearer her shoulders, and cuddled her. Bits of sand clung to his cheeks, and she brushed it off.

"I would've stayed in the water longer," he declared.

"Uh, huh." She still shivered, but the heat of the fire, the warmth of Colum's body, offered pure pleasure. "Then why are your lips blue?"

"Yours are bluer." A relaxed smile worked across his

features. She recalled how his eyes darkened whenever he'd contemplated kissing her after a swim, and her pulse quickened. The scent of salt water and his damp skin brought wants and misgivings.

He bent his head, cupped her face and kissed her with aching tenderness. Oh, the taste of him, the gentleness of an unstoppable kiss. She didn't want it to end—like their youthful declarations. Only her emotions were different now. Deeper and sounder.

She pressed her forehead against his chest, her hands flattened on his shoulders. "I wish you could stay in Wexford permanently," she whispered. "This is your home."

"For many years, but not anymore." He gathered a deep breath. "In all honesty, I can't risk being hurt again."

"You're referring to me?"

"Aye."

She blinked, focusing on his words. "I wouldn't do that." She drew back, attempting to understand the overwhelming emotions he awakened in her. Had she hidden behind outward merriment and animation in London—a vigilant emotional balance that numbed her feelings? She'd clung to that balance for years, thankful for her two cherished daughters to love and care for.

"I realize you wouldn't intentionally." Colum kissed her forehead. "Though, please understand that my heart can only take so much."

She went to stand, and he kept his arm firmly around her. "May I hold you a while longer?"

Why? He'd hedged about continuing their relationship. Maybe he'd never been interested. Still, his affectionate smile melted her insides, and she relaxed. She regarded him and fingered the greying hairs at his temple. His lashes were black and spiky, his features well-defined.

She stirred, and he drew her closer, and the instinctively

protective gesture prompted her to smile. He buried his face in her hair, and she leaned back and briefly squeezed her eyes closed. Two people reconnecting on a windswept Irish beach. Two sweethearts. Tonight, she felt wholly at peace with herself, and in seamless accord with the universe.

"There's a family of otters. I saw them earlier when I took a swim. And kingfishers." He pointed toward the water, a sheet of indigo-blue silk. The moon rose higher, reflecting a milky glow across the hills. A chorus of crickets and the sizzling pops of the fire serenaded them, the murmurs of the departing guests fading away. "Do you recall when we'd spend the day intent on spotting an otter?"

"Aye. You'd spin their water frolics into fairy tales." Her throat clogged with tears. She inhaled a deep breath to compose herself.

"Once upon a time," he'd often recited in their youth, *"there was a girl named Kiki, and a guy named Colum."*

A fairytale. A happily ever after.

What happiness had she missed while she'd worn blinders —all to achieve success in a fickle career?

THE FOLLOWING morning dawned pleasant and clear. Keira drew open her lace curtains and gazed out her second-floor bedroom window, smirking as her mum directed the workers on the placement of the large white tent and the cathedral windows on the sidewalls. Colum's father guided other workmen on the location of the portable heaters.

Further down the shore, Colum emerged from the water. His swimming trunks draped low on his hips, his muscular chest glistened with drops of water. The sun glinted behind him, outlining his athletic physique.

He slung a towel around his neck and padded over to their parents.

Watching him, Keira's thoughts emptied of everything except him.

He raised his head, as if he felt her gaze.

"Aren't you chilly?" she teased.

He gave a look of lighthearted superiority. "Not a bit."

"You aren't serious. The temperature of the water is fifty degrees Fahrenheit."

"In truth, I'm frozen."

Her shout of hilarity almost drowned out his next remark.

"Can't wait to see what you'll wear to the wedding, Kiki," he said.

Kiki again.

She ignored the unexpected knot in her chest. Or, at least, she tried. A memory of their mutual years flashed through her mind—holding hands at sunset, shared secrets in the dark. Despite her anticipation of an exciting lifestyle beyond Wexford, she couldn't pretend the flood of emotions whenever he was near didn't exist.

"It'll bring tears to your eyes," she called back.

She assumed she'd moved on with her life. She hadn't. For decades, she'd searched to fill the void in her heart. And she'd fallen in love, once again, with the man she'd left behind.

An hour later, Keira donned a knee-length, carnation red dress with a polka-dotted sash that she'd fashioned and sewn. The ends of her hair boasted a ruby hue, and she styled her heavy curls to the side with a pearl clip. She opted for braided jute sandals, satisfied that her outfit was tasteful and sensible.

As she gazed at her reflection in her full-length mirror, she recalled the conversation with her mum from the previous evening, after Keira and Colum had parted.

She'd knocked on Keira's bedroom door and entered. "I wanted to speak to you about Colum," she'd begun. "Day in and day out through the years, you looked splendid as a couple, but especially tonight."

"We're great friends."

"So you've made known. Nonetheless, I see the way he looks at you."

"I haven't noticed anything of the sort," Keira had replied.

"He can't stop staring, and you dissolve whenever you meet his gaze."

"He's leaving in mere days."

"Encourage him to stay. You've never gotten over each other. The sooner you both admit the truth, the better."

Her mother had known how difficult it was for Keira to leave him and Wexford all those decades ago. It hadn't been an easy decision.

"He has work and obligations in Farthing," Keira replied.

Even now, she longed for the tenderness of his embrace, the gentle insistence of his kiss. She'd appreciated the precious hours they'd spent in each other's company, and she sensed Colum felt the same. But what would tomorrow evening bring? Or the following? Would they finally celebrate a New Year's side by side again?

All those decades ago, she'd departed the day after Christmas, intent on securing a flat in London before her modeling contract began the first of January.

"New Year's is symbolic, Kiki," Colum had explained. They'd spent every holiday never more than a stone's throw from each other. *"Let's reflect on the past year, then look forward."*

By the time they were teens, they'd toasted, their sparkling grape juice glasses clinking as they cozied in Colum's living room by a fire in the hearth, while their parents celebrated at the local pub. They'd return well before midnight and switch the television on for a communal countdown.

"Why do folks insist on coming in the front door, then leaving out the back door?" Keira had asked him.

"It's touted to bring good luck." His lips had deepened into an exasperated smile. *"Another one of Ireland's traditions."*

Laughing, she'd refuted, *"Many traditions have a purpose behind them. Rituals are performed for hundreds of years, although few folks can recall why."*

His look implied a struggle between seriousness and humor. *"Here's a tradition that will last. Come what may, we'll spend New Year's with one another every year."*

Keira blinked back tears at the remembrance. That was the last New Year's she'd seen him.

"Sometimes the pathway to the person you cherish is a twisty and lengthy road," her mum was saying. Her eyes had misted, although her smile offered encouragement.

Keira snapped up her bouquet, a fragrant mix of snapdragons and sunflowers, then walked to the window. Laughing and chatting, in a kaleidoscope of vibrant dresses and navy suits, ushers were seating the guests in rows of white chairs facing the sea. The pastor fixed himself at the altar, a classic wooden archway decorated with purple sea asters.

Her veins tingled with excitement at the enthusiasm of the guests. Today was a glorious, sunny day, the rugged landscape dusted with snow on the highest mountain peaks. The stark blue skies promised joyfulness and enchantment.

At noon, the ceremony began with a lone bagpiper playing Mendelssohn's Wedding March. A ripple went through the crowd as Keira and Colum took their places, and the bride walked down the aisle to her groom.

Her mum's champagne lace dress complemented her rosy complexion. The flowered crown headpiece brought a statement of romance to her wavy gray hair. Her closely set blue eyes brimmed with happiness.

Colum's father, dressed in a black notched tuxedo, stood ruddy faced and noble, beaming as his bride approached.

Keira gazed at the two men, father and son. Their resemblance was astounding. The square jawlines and eye color were the same, as were their natures. Attentive and charismatic, both men forever wore a smile.

"You're beautiful," Colum said softly to her. His green eyes glistened with tears.

Her stomach flipped and she smiled—craving all things Colum. The boy he was, and the man he'd become.

Behind him, the sea shimmered—sparkles under the sun. In her teens, she'd imagined the shimmers as magical fairy dust, and that the magic would lead to an enchanted life with him.

After the wedding, they'd sing and dance at the reception. The lively melody of Galway Girl, an Irish tune. Or a romantic waltz, and he'd hold her in his arms.

Her pulse thrummed with the anticipation of another day with him.

She'd suggest he stay a wee bit longer. She wanted him to meet her daughters. She was so proud of them.

"All Those Endearing Young Charms," closed the ceremony. The emotional lyrics about a woman's youth fading away, encouraged the guests to join in.

Dozens offered congratulations, circling the bride and groom as they stepped toward the tent. Traditional Irish pub fare—hearty fish and chips, shepherd's pie, and seafood chowder, would be served buffet-style.

Keira caught up to Colum, who was speaking on his cellphone. His eyebrows crinkled in concern.

"Are you coming?" she asked.

He clicked off the phone. "I can't. I must leave."

"Now?"

"The young man in Farthing I told you about—"

"Sean? You loaded up his refrigerator."

Colum rubbed his jaw. "He hit a rough patch and was thrown out of his flat."

"He recently moved in."

"Correct, but he needs me. Patrick Gervez and his wife, Cora, are also in Farthing. They flew over from America for a visit to Ireland in the wintertime."

"Can't they handle Sean's problems?"

"They're on holiday. They're good friends, but Sean is my responsibility."

"He really isn't."

"He is, though." Colum's tone was strained, his chin high. "I won't shirk my obligation and ask my American friends to shoulder my burdens. I'll extend my congratulatory wishes to our parents and go pack."

What obligation? she thought. You're not even technically related. I need you too.

She respected that Colum always placed the welfare of others before himself, but she wanted him to be a part of her life too.

"Then . . . this is goodbye?" she asked aloud.

"Kiki, I've been thinking. Maybe it's better this way." He strode closer, his gaze locked on hers. "Our friendship has lasted decades, and neither of us can ignore our first love. But we shouldn't complicate our relationship with anything else."

Like romance? Like love? Like kisses under the moonlight?

Her vision blurred, her chest ached. "Aye. Friends till the end." She swiveled. She wouldn't let him see her cry. Keeping her shoulders straight, she quickened her pace to the tent.

She remained out of sight when Colum got into his car a

few minutes later. He'd changed into jeans and a button down blue shirt, and shrugged on a jacket. For a moment he waffled, glancing around.

"I'm right here," she was tempted to shout. But she didn't, and the stab of regret pierced deeper as he drove away. She'd never see his lopsided smile, nor hear his easy-going chuckle, again.

HER MUM APPEARED—KEIRA wasn't sure when.

"He left early because someone needed him." Tears clogged Keira's throat. She trembled, despite the sun's warmth.

"He apologized for his hasty departure. He always was the first in line to come to everyone else's aid." She gave Keira's hand a mild squeeze. "You'll see him again."

When? Keira's fingers were cold, but her mum didn't seem to mind.

CHAPTER 6

Two weeks later, and the day after Christmas, Colum flicked warning glances at his four-year-old ballerina students, but they paid him no heed. They knew he was a marshmallow when it came to disciplining them. Dressed in pink tights and black leotards, their hair tugged back in classic buns, they raced around his studio like it was a preschool gym. They should've been practicing their pitter patter turns by the barre. Instead, they practiced . . . running.

He clapped his hands to bring their attention to him. Alas, no such luck. He hunkered down to tie a tiny ballet slipper, reminded them to work at their dances for the upcoming recital, and then shepherded them to their waiting parents.

After speaking assurances to several anxious mothers, and thanking them for bringing their children for a last-minute practice, he arranged his gear in his locker and leaned his head against the wall. Since resuming his everyday life, he'd grown weary of the town of Farthing—and even his surrogate nephew.

After attending a morning church service the day before, their Christmas dinner had consisted of takeout boxty,

243

potato pancakes stuffed with meat and vegetables. For the remainder of the day, Colum had volunteered at a soup kitchen while his nephew created a custom logo for a local shop.

In addition, Colum's dreams had started again—driving on a shadowy road and being lost.

He grasped a cigarette, then shoved it back into his pocket. He craved a coffee, or tea . . . but he'd have to sit in traffic forever first. In Wexford, everything was a mere ten minutes away.

"*I dine at Michael D's often,*" Keira had declared.

Keira—eternally in his heart, eternally in his mind. He'd assumed he was over her. He'd assumed he'd secured her in a safe, secret place. Returning to Wexford had been bittersweet, but memories of her and their years together had struck him at every turn. He'd even jogged along the beach the morning after his arrival and discovered the oak tree where they'd carved their initials when they were twelve.

But in a forty-eight-hour period, how could he reunite with his teenage sweetheart? He was a bachelor in his fifties and wasn't about to leave everything he'd worked so hard for, to move back to his hometown. Plus, could he truly contemplate settling down?

He blew out a breath. He'd tried to forget her. If anything, his feelings had grown stronger.

With a cheery nod to the straggling parents, he shrugged on his twill jacket and exited the studio.

Restless, he wandered the bustling city streets as people hurried home from work. Bright icicle lights illuminated the shops, and aromatic pine filled the air. Daylight had dwindled, and a purple dusk came earlier than expected. The days, the years, passed too quickly, and each hour was precious.

He paused. So what was he doing in Farthing?

He'd told himself not to care, citing a myriad of reasons, expecting his feelings would fade.

She'd left at eighteen, and he'd been devastated. Nevertheless, he loved her—a love so powerful it exploded within him. Surely, she felt the same.

He needed to take the right path and find his way home. Back to Keira and Wexford.

He drew out his cellphone to contact his father, then Keira's mum.

He hesitated.

Texts were a start. In person was better.

Decision made, he rang Sean, and offered his flat to sublet. Colum had secured a part-time job to enable Sean to get his finances in order and hoped the lad would be responsible. He'd shared his knowledge and been a sounding board. Now was a chance for the young man to transition to independence.

Then Colum enlisted the help of his father and Keira's mum.

Next came a phone call to Patrick Gervez and his wife, Cora, inviting them to visit the southern part of Ireland and Colum's hometown for a special event.

His fourth request was to Clara, his employer and long-time friend. She assured she'd find a suitable teacher replacement, that the recital would go off without a hitch, and encouraged Colum to follow his heart.

His heart. He pressed a hand to his chest.

He hurried to his flat to attend to last-minute details and pack a suitcase.

Then he drove to Wexford as if his life depended on it.

CHAPTER 7

*K*eira wrapped her fingers around a fresh mug of tea, leaned back in the oversized Adirondack chair on the O'Brien's lawn, and gazed at the blue-grey ripples of the water, a reflection of the sky. Today, she wore a one-piece V-neck jumpsuit, a snuggly knit in a bold fuchsia, and draped a thick woolen cape over her shoulders to ward off the chill.

The end of December carried a chilly, overcast day, and the holiday had occurred in a blur. Colum had texted every day—and they'd kept the topics neutral.

After a Christmas church service in town, she'd prepared roast turkey, stuffing, and buttery carrots, and dined with their parents. Colum had phoned, wishing them all a "Merry Christmas." He'd perfected his friendly, amiable tone.

Her eyes burned, but she didn't blame it on the smoke from the turf fires.

She blamed it on the tears she'd shed since he'd departed. All that remained were precious snapshots of their youth that she safeguarded in her mind. Many years ago, he'd unknowingly set the bar high. His likable character, wit, and intelligence had become the standard she'd unwittingly measured every man by since. They were so compatible—pieces of a puzzle fitting in perfect agreement.

"Hello, Kiki, my love," a deep, beloved voice came from behind her.

She gasped. The shattering gentleness of Colum's words sent a jolt through her.

She set her mug on the grass and slowly rose. Now he stood in front of her—his tall frame clad in dark jeans, a flannel shirt, and his familiar twill jacket. She assumed she was still breathing. She couldn't be sure.

"Colum." Her thoughts reeled. His presence was a solid force, mesmeric and undeniable. "Why . . . why are you here?"

"I missed you." His tone was whispered, raw with emotion. "And, I'm here to stay. Do you know any place for rent?"

"In Wexford?" Her gaze lifted to the man who held her heart. "For whatever reason?"

"For you. Only for you." He captured her in his arms. His lips pressed hungrily with an aching desire that would forever remain in her memory.

She molded nearer to him. "I've missed you too." Their breaths mingled. She returned his kiss with all the yearning in her soul.

His hands slid up and down her back. "I came to tell you that I love you. Everything you do—everything you say—everything you represent."

The taste of his lips brought unbearable happiness. She didn't want him to stop, fearful he might disappear.

"My precious Kiki, you're goodness, decency, and all that's true in the world," he said. "You're the treasure of my life."

She pressed a trembling finger to his mouth. "And you're

the treasure of mine." Heat radiated through her body. Her heartbeat raced so loud, surely he heard it.

Tears glistened at the corner of his eyes as he kept her firmly in his embrace. "I was fearful of having my heart broken anew and ordered myself not to love you."

She wiped away his tears. "And?"

"It didn't work." He cradled her face in his hands. "When we were apart, I realized we'd missed out on love once, and I won't allow it to happen again."

"I can't believe you're here. I'm speechless."

"All I need is a single word." He pulled a small black velvet box from his pocket and handed it to her.

She opened the box, which revealed a sterling Claddagh ring. "When did you—?"

"The ring is your mum's. She's a grand woman."

Keira ran her palm along the gleaming silver. The crown symbolized loyalty, friendship, and the heart represented love. Tenderness pulsed through her. He'd returned, determined to recover the love they'd begun decades earlier.

"Do you like it?" In his eagerness, his features appeared almost boyish.

"Nothing can ever mean more."

"If you don't . . . I'll buy you a new ring, although it's bad luck."

"You don't believe in Irish folklore."

"I'm changing my mind about many beliefs, especially if it ensures your happiness."

His response made her throat ache. Her Colum, ever wanting to please her.

"The ring is perfect," she said.

"Keira Moira Murphy." Colum brushed his lips over her forehead, her cheeks, her mouth. "Will you marry me?"

"I can't wait to be your wife." She looped her fingers

around his nape. Her lips parted for his lengthy, loving kiss. "Aye. Aye. Aye."

"Let's plan a New Year's Eve wedding, if you agree."

"New Year's is only a few days from now."

"That'll do."

"Our engagement will last less than a week?"

"Our engagement has survived decades." He glanced at her cottage. "We'll make our home there."

"You'll be living with me?"

"When we're married. Aye. A place next door to our parents is ideal, as we can care for them as they grow older. We have a responsibility to ensure they are secure, protected, and we're providing the help they may require."

"It's more than a responsibility. I consider it a privilege."

"Well stated. Plus, it's convenient whenever your recipes call for a cup of sugar." He winked.

"I don't bake. I sew."

"So we'll dine at Michael D's a lot."

She smiled. "A definite improvement over my cooking."

"I remember you were never much of a cook."

"What else do you remember?"

"I recall you always fired my heart into a tailspin." He tossed her one of his lopsided smiles. "And, I remembered the vacant building in town. I located the owner, and I've secured a lease on the place adjacent to your shop. This little town needs more culture and a community theater is an excellent beginning."

"You mentioned you preferred bigger cities."

He quirked an eyebrow. "Can a man adjust his opinions, or is that a woman's prerogative?"

"Both." She laughed. "Colum O'Brien, you've made me so happy."

"Kiki, I've only just begun."

EPILOGUE

*N*ew Year's Eve day brought a brisk breeze and threat of showers. Outside, a huge white tent had been erected near the Irish Sea, and both the ceremony and reception would be held inside. Large propane portable heaters had been set up to take away the bite in the air.

Keira gave a last glance at herself in the mirror at her light-peach lace wedding dress, pleased with her appearance. The ivory netting veil with a feather and tulle flower; accented the feminine, flowing lines. She'd dipped the ends of her hair in a subtle shade of dusty yellow.

At two o'clock, the ceremony opened with the swell of keyboard music, and a hush went through the crowd. The tent glowed with candlelight, perfumed with rich bouquets of shamrock and crimson roses, tied with red satin ribbons. She savored every second, giving a special nod to her two beautiful daughters and her new friends, Patrick and Cora Gervez.

Colum had introduced her to them when they'd arrived from Farthing for the wedding, and they'd immediately invited her and Colum to America—enthusiastically chatting about their colleagues and family in Bloomingfield, California.

"You'll enjoy Julie Rossi's restaurant, The Pasta Junction, because she makes her own homemade pasta every day," Cora had gushed, as she tucked a dark-brown curl behind her ear. "Her husband, Lorenzo, is the local weatherman."

'We work together at the television studio." Patrick's blue eyes gleamed with pride as he beamed down at his wife.

Keira and Colum assured they'd love to see America.

"Perhaps for our honeymoon?" Colum asked her. "January weather in California is mild and has it all—beaches, mountains, and, from what Patrick has described—Bloomingfield Candy Shop—the finest chocolate shop in the world."

"Aye, it sounds grand," she'd replied.

As Keira started down the aisle, she carried a photo in her mind of this day—her true wedding day, exquisite and with the promise of a lifetime of love.

When she approached the altar, she grinned at her mum, her matron of honor, and Colum's father, the best man.

Then her gaze locked with her tall, handsome groom, resplendent in a dove-gray suit and emerald-green tie that matched his eyes.

Colum gazed at her with quiet joy. "Hello, my love," he whispered.

She recalled everything they'd been through, their decades apart. Love had emerged from friendship and taken hold. In harmony, their journey had led them back to exactly where they'd begun, and truly, this was the happiest of New Year's. Welcoming the future and letting go of the past, in the company of her loved ones.

With her hands laced with his, she repeated her wedding vows with him. They commenced the ceremony by reciting a traditional Irish blessing, an ancient Celtic prayer:

"May the road rise up to meet you.

May the wind be always at your back.

May the sun shine warm upon your face; the rains fall soft upon your fields and until we meet again, may God hold you in the palm of His hand."

And then she silently added to herself:

Once upon a time, there was a girl named Kiki, and a guy named Colum.

A fairytale. A happily ever after.

THE END

RECIPE FOR CHERYL'S IRISH SODA BREAD

Ingredients:

2 1/2 cups all-purpose flour

3 tablespoons sugar

2 teaspoons baking powder

1 teaspoon baking soda

1/2 teaspoon salt

1/3 cup cold butter, cut into chunks

1/2 cup currants or raisins

1 1/4 cups buttermilk

Substitute 4 teaspoons vinegar or lemon juice plus enough milk to equal 1 1/4 cups. Let stand 5 minutes.

Preparation:

STEP 1

Heat oven to 375°F. Line baking sheet with parchment paper; set aside.

STEP 2

Combine all ingredients except buttermilk and currants in bowl; cut in butter until mixture resembles coarse crumbs. Stir in buttermilk and currants just until moistened.

STEP 3

Turn dough onto lightly floured surface; knead gently 10 times. Shape into a ball. Place onto the prepared baking sheet. Pat into 6-inch circle. Cut 1/2 inch deep "X" in top of dough with sharp knife.

STEP 4

Bake 30-35 minutes or until golden brown. Serve warm. Enjoy!

A NOTE FROM JOSIE

Dear Reader,

Thank you for reading *A Chocolate-Box Irish Wedding*.

I wanted to write another story loosely connected to the "Chocolate-Box" series, and set the story in Ireland during the holidays and New Year's. I chose Colum, a character from Oh Danny Boy and also brought two characters from A Chocolate-Box Christmas Wish—Cora and Patrick—to share a winter romance with you.

If you loved this sweet romance as much as I loved writing it, please help other people find *A Chocolate-Box Irish Wedding* by posting your review.

A Chocolate-Box Irish Wedding is available in ebook, paperback, Large Print paperback, Hardcover, and audiobook.

My Spotify Play List for A Chocolate-Box Irish Wedding is here.

Love sweet romance holiday stories?

Be sure to check out the book bundles:

Holiday Hearts Volume One

Holiday Hearts Volume Two

Holiday Hearts Book Bundle Volume Three
Holiday Hearts Volume Four

Love the Chocolate-Box sweet romances?
Be sure to check out all the books in this series:
Click here.

ABOUT THE AUTHOR

Josie Riviera is a *USA TODAY* bestselling author of contemporary, inspirational, and historical sweet romances that read like Hallmark movies. She lives in the Charlotte, NC, area with her wonderfully supportive husband. They share their home with an adorable shih tzu, who constantly needs grooming, and live in an old house forever needing renovations.

Become a member of my Read and Review VIP Facebook group for exclusive giveaways and ARCs.

To connect with Josie, visit her webpage and subscribe to her newsletter. As a thank-you, she'll send you a free sweet romance novella directly to your inbox.

josieriviera.com

ALSO BY JOSIE RIVIERA

Seeking Patience

Seeking Catherine (always Free!)

Seeking Fortune

Seeking Charity

Seeking Rachel

The Seeking Series

Oh Danny Boy

I Love You More

A Snowy White Christmas

A Portuguese Christmas

Holiday Hearts Book Bundle Volume One

Holiday Hearts Book Bundle Volume Two

Holiday Hearts Book Bundle Volume Three

Holiday Hearts Book Bundle Volume Four

Candleglow and Mistletoe

Maeve (Perfect Match)

A Love Song To Cherish

A Christmas To Cherish

A Valentine To Cherish

A Christmas Puppy To Cherish

A Homecoming To Cherish

A Summer To Cherish

Romance Stories To Cherish

Romance Stories To Cherish Volume Two

Cherished Hearts Six Book Volume

Aloha To Love

Sweet Peppermint Kisses

Valentine Hearts Boxed Set

1-800-CUPID

1-800-CHRISTMAS

1-800-IRELAND

1-800-SUMMER

1-800-NEW YEAR

The 1-800-Series Sweet Contemporary Romance Bundle

Irish Hearts Sweet Romance Bundle

Holly's Gift

A Chocolate-Box Christmas

A Chocolate-Box New Years

A Chocolate-Box Valentine

A Chocolate-Box Summer Breeze

A Chocolate-Box Christmas Wish

A Chocolate-Box Irish Wedding

Chocolate-Box Hearts

Chocolate-Box Hearts Volume Two

Chocolate-Box Double Hearts

Recipes From The Heart

Leading Hearts

New Year Hearts

SENIOR HEARTS

Summer Hearts

Christmas in the Air (1-800-Book)

A Very Christian Christmas

The 1-800-Series Volume Two

The 1-800-Series Complete

Christmas Tails of the Heart

Pawfect Christmas Hearts

Most books are available in ebook, audiobook, paperback, Large Print paperback and Hardcover.

Many are FREE on Kindle Unlimited!